Sophie would never forgive Dad for telling her in front of people, leaving her nowhere to move. There was no way to make up her own version. No way to pretend it wasn't happening and didn't matter. She could not call her sister and talk it through, or pick up a brick and throw it at Dad and hope he was scarred for life.

Sophie tried to stare her father down, but he was not looking at her. He had not looked at her in weeks. He saw only Persia.

How quickly it had happened. As fast as a computer crashing, that fast had her parents' marriage gone down.

Tune In Anytime

Caroline B. Cooney

Published by
Dell Laurel-Leaf
an imprint of
Random House Children's Books
a division of Random House, Inc.
1540 Broadway
New York, New York 10036

Visit us on the Web! www.randomhouse.com/teens

**Educators and librarians, for a variety of teaching
tools, visit us at www.randomhouse.com/teachers**

ISBN: 0-440-22798-4
RL: 5.7
Reprinted by arrangement with Delacorte Press
Printed in the United States of America
July 2001

10 9 8 7 6 5 4 3 2
OPM

How to star in a soap opera.

There are probably many ways to break into soap operas, but one way, Sophie discovered, is just to stand there. As your parents lose their minds, their sense and their money, you will be the star. The one around whom all the action pivots. This will be a show you cannot quit. A script you cannot rewrite. You will be stuck on the set, surrounded by bad lines and bad actors. Every morning, you will say, "No more episodes! End this!"

But in a soap opera, there is always another episode.

By the time Sophie Olivette realized that she was a star in her own soap, the action had been going on for some time. She just hadn't had the TV on. Or she'd been watching some other channel.

It was as if Sophie's father walked in, grabbed the remote and turned up the volume.

Chapter 1

Sophie loved the sound of her father in the house, and when she heard him bounding up the stairs, she hopped off the bed where she and Jem and Ash were sitting to paint each other's nails. She had so much to tell him. It had been the kind of school day where everything explodes— Sophie had whipped the history exam, given her first ever speech (without even throwing up), been awesome in field hockey, and now she had incredible fingertips.

The carpeting on the stair and the upper hall was thick and nubbly. It had muffled the sound of a second pair of feet.

Sophie grabbed the doorjamb to stop her momentum. She could not fling herself on top of her father, nor order him to sit quietly and listen to her brilliant three-minute A-plus speech. His arms were full, and *he* was the one about to deliver a speech.

No, thought Sophie. Please, no.

She was not addressing her father, but some Power that ought to protect marriage.

But her father was bursting. "Sophie!" he cried joyfully. "Persia and I," he told his daughter, "are getting married."

Jem and Ash were still holding their fingers stiffly and separately, like children about to trace around their hands. They sat on the bed, right behind Sophie, and heard every word and saw every gesture.

Sophie would never forgive Dad for telling her in front of people, leaving her nowhere to move. There was no way to make up her own version. No way to pretend it wasn't happening and didn't matter. She could not call her sister and talk it through, or pick up a brick and throw it at Dad and hope he was scarred for life.

Sophie tried to stare her father down, but he was not looking at her. He had not looked at her in weeks. He saw only Persia.

How quickly it had happened. As fast as a computer crashing, that fast had her parents' marriage gone down.

Only two months before, Sophie's happily married parents had been proud and nervous: their older daughter, Marley, was going off to college.

Marley was one of those capable, competent people who stride across rooms and life and get what they want on the first try, mostly by stepping on other people. Sharing a life, a house and a high school with Marley was exhausting. That last week of summer, when Mother and Dad drove away with Marley and her million possessions, Sophie had twirled around the empty house, clapping and yelling, "Marley's not here!" and then falling down on her bed laughing.

Life without Marley! It was a beautiful thought.

At college, however, Marley faced a problem. She was assigned a roommate. Marley was not a roommate kind of person. People who must get their own way are difficult to live with in a space ten feet by twelve feet.

The only kind of roommate that would have worked for Marley would have been the submissive, doormat kind. The kind who said, "Oh, Marley, please let me fold your laundry too."

Instead, Marley got Persia, who was a few years older, having been a model before starting college. Marley, sharpened by years of bickering with her sister, expected to control Persia.

And what had Persia expected? A regular old freshman year?

Sophie could have asked, but she and Persia were not on speaking terms. Only Sophie knew this, because Persia had a great capacity for not noticing other people's emotions. Persia was untouched by irritation or anger or even homicidal threats.

In any event, after only ten days of college, Marley decided to come home for the weekend.

Invoking some ancient rule that roomies could always go home with roommates, Persia came too.

The rest was history.

Family history was supposed to be a fun thing, full of interesting ancestors who arrived on American shores in exciting ways. Family history should not happen to Sophie.

And now her father had closed up their lives in one sentence. The vision of his future made him so happy he had to say it again, in a rich round voice, as if repeating wedding vows. "Persia and I," he said proudly, "are getting married."

"You aren't single," said Sophie. Because he was skipping an important fact. If he and Persia were getting married . . . first, he must divorce Mother.

Sophie could not look at her own personal father—a man who should be off-limits if there ever was one—holding hands with Persia. She slammed the door. "Never!" she yelled. "Never, never, never, never, never, *never in this world.*"

Her scream, magnificent though it was, gave her a fierce spinal-tap headache, like a viciously cold swallow of crushed ice.

Out in the hall, Persia did not seem to notice that there was now a solid wood door between them. "Sophie," she cried, "Daniel and I are planning our wedding. Of course we want you to be a bridesmaid. Marley will be the maid of honor, since she introduced us."

"Honor?" yelled Sophie. "Where do you find honor when you cheat on your marriage! And I will never be in your wedding! I'll kill you first. How do you want to die? Fire? Bombs? Car crashes?" She was hammering on her own door, as if *they* had locked *her* out.

"Now, Sophie," said her father, as if the topic was skipping vegetables in favor of dessert. "Do you have any idea where your mother is? I really should tell her, too."

Ash put a hand over her mouth, hiding shock. Jem appeared to be securing anything that might be used as a murder weapon.

"It's okay," Sophie told them. "I won't kill Dad and Persia while you're here. You won't have to testify or anything." She was horrified to find that she could actually imagine killing him. She could feel the weapon in her hand. Stop this, she said to herself. You don't want your own father dead.

But it would be fine if Persia hit a slick spot in the road.

"We'll be accessories because we know you're plotting homicide," said Jem, giggling nervously.

"A special kind of homicide," Ash pointed out. "A patricide."

It sounded quite elegant when you said *patricide*. As honorable as being a bridesmaid. How dare her father talk of weddings? What about his original wedding vows? Vows that were still in effect.

Then came the twin sounds of their footsteps departing. First they dared descend upon her bedroom, in her end of the house, and throw that in her face? And now they dared walk away?

Sophie wrenched the door open, slamming it backward so hard the knob crunched into her bedroom wall. She stormed after them. "How dare you tell me first?" she shrieked. "You can't be bothered to tell your own wife?"

"Soph, I would have, but she's out. Didn't she go somewhere to commune with the spirits?"

"Stones," said Persia. "She's speaking to stones, she was very clear about that when she dashed out." Together, Persia and Sophie's father laughed at Sophie's mother.

The way they laughed at Sophie's mother sounded as if they did it routinely. It was more awful than anything. More awful than imagining sex between them.

Edith Olivette was a woman of passions. In her search for truth and meaning, she had been through astrology, crystals, tai chi, bird-watching, pottery, playing the lute, bingo, and poetry. Sophie enjoyed her mother's passions. They tended to be short-term. Six months was a long time for Edith. Her current passion was Ancient People, and the harmony of mind, body and earth they had known and we had forgotten.

Along her passionate way, Mother had forgotten a few things herself—such as fashion, hair, punctuality, checkbook balancing and shopping. Mother had, in fact, become somewhat odd.

Needless to say, Dad and Mother had grown apart.

Mother was confused and hurt. She continued

to adore Dad. She could not understand why he complained so much. He wanted her to dress better, accessorize better, wear makeup again, have her hair done, be a good hostess and entertain his guests. "But you do such a lovely job at that!" Mother would cry. "We have an excellent division of labor."

"We haven't divided the labor at all!" Dad would shout. "I'm doing everything. You're too busy with your Inner Self to contribute. I want a wife who understands why I'm working so hard, and what I've built."

"I'm working equally hard," Mother would tell him. "It's just difficult to see improvements and additions to the inner soul."

Right now, Mother's inner soul was focused on the winter solstice, a holiday she had recently discovered. Other people might approach the coming of chilly weather by thinking of Thanksgiving or Christmas. Indeed, for her previous forty-five years, Mother had spent much time and thought on these. This year, however, they were as nothing. Mother worried exclusively about the crossing of planets and stars and the dire possibility that she might not be in the right place at the right time on December twenty-first.

It did look as if Mother would be in the wrong place.

Dad was going to divorce her and marry a twenty-one-year-old.

On soap operas, time stretches and molds itself. A scene that takes only moments in real time lasts Monday through Friday in soap-opera time. Conversations and glances go on for days.

There are no grown-ups in a soap opera. If people behaved like grown-ups, there would be no action.

Sophie found herself in a world without grown-ups.

Chapter 2

Daniel Olivette was house-crazy. Not satisfied with an immense house that had won architectural awards and been in *House Beautiful,* he'd added a tower. Attached to the rest of the house by a sunroom filled with ferns, it featured a baking kitchen on the first floor with an impressive brick French oven; a guest suite on the second floor, with views of the city skyline; and on the third floor, a room of glass. A spy tower, from which you could gaze upon weather and birds and planes and the ever-interesting activities of neighbors.

It was the neighbors who were watching the Olivettes now, for Persia had moved into the guest suite.

Sophie caught up to them in the fern room, where damp green fronds and the sinister stems of orchids brushed against her. Her father was such a handsome man. Tall, slim and distinguished; always dressed right, as if he were a consultant for a catalog: what to wear on every occasion—the beach, the opera, the divorce.

The desire to kill him evaporated.

Sophie loved him, and she felt within herself a great store of patience and understanding. She would draw him back, make him see. A person who could give a speech such as the one she had given today could accomplish anything with words. "Dad," she said, "you can't do this." She felt the strength of her argument; the absolute truth of it. It was like gravity or velocity. "You must not do this," she explained.

Her father seemed genuinely bewildered. "Sophie, honey," he said, "you can't expect me to stay with your mother."

Of course she expected him to stay.

That was what parents did. They stayed.

Other families might divorce, but your own family—never.

She wanted to hug him. She wanted to be his little girl; be all the little girls she had ever been: the two-year-old, the ten-year-old. But he had his arms around Persia, and the two of them were a castle wall. She could not break through.

"Anyway," her father added, "Edith is just a pyramidiot."

Sophie had never heard the word *pyramidiot*. It was cruel and true. Pyramids were a previous passion of Mother's, part of an Egyptian kick that had resulted in maps of the Nile, a bust of Nefertiti and assorted books on mummies. These could be found gathering dust next to last year's bird guides or hidden beneath new books on comprehending the cosmos.

Only this morning Edith had learned that up in a meadow across the town was an ancient stone circle. A real Stonehenge! Here in America! Edith dashed out to see. She told her husband where she was going; she even told Persia. You would have thought that Persia was still her daughter's college roommate, just here for pizza.

Sophie was shocked now at the extent to which she and her mother had pretended this was not happening.

I should have tied Persia up with duct tape, thought Sophie. Kicked her around for a while. Driven her back to that stupid college and dumped her on the green grass in front of her dorm. Kicked her a little more. So what if it's assault and battery? Better a light jail sentence than a divorce.

Divorce.

The word was horrible, with that splitting-up *v* in the middle of it; that going-in-two-directions *v*.

If Dad actually did this; if he actually married Persia; he would force upon Sophie and Marley and their mother the most profound event of their lives since birth. And next to that pronouncement, how pointless other topics were. Sophie was never going to be able to brag about her explosions of success—field hockey, history, public speaking. No point in mentioning that dance tryouts were tomorrow.

"After all Edith's nonsense," said her father, "I need reason and intelligence."

As if reason and intelligence attracted him to Persia. Talk about a trophy wife. Persia was perfect for the part. She was beautiful in a thin gold breakable way, like a tree ornament. But she would last. Someone would always wrap her carefully.

"Besides, I'm tired of this house," her father went on. "It represents the Past. Persia and I are going to enter Our Marriage as Travelers. Our New Life will have no geographic center. We will tour the world from Paris to Egypt to India."

Twenty-one years of marriage? And eight weeks was enough to talk in capital letters of a New Life with a New Wife?

"We will not," said her father grandly, "be hobbled by convention or tradition."

"Then why do you want a wedding and bridesmaids?" said Sophie, who heard enough capital-letter talk from Mother.

Mother's whole existence was Travel. Her search for the Path. The necessity to Lose the Baggage of Previous Journeys, so she could Travel Light into a New Life.

Just last week, Ash and Jem had amused themselves by drawing up a list of passions that Sophie's Mother had not yet fallen into. Collecting Elvis memorabilia, suggested Ash. Raising free-range chickens and selling eggs, said Jem.

Sophie had thought: What if one day Mother travels so lightly she doesn't even need me?

Wrong. It was Dad who didn't need his family.

"So I'm selling the house," said Dad, as casually as if this meant selling a lawn chair or a magazine subscription.

Sophie felt sick and dizzy. This place into which Dad had poured his every dollar and hope? Their wonderful tower and mansion—sold? Her suite, with its glass-fronted bookcases, three walk-in closets and bathroom with skylights? Their entertainment room, with its separate screen for movies, reclining chairs and special sound system?

Persia gave Dad a shimmering smile. What kind of name was Persia, anyway? It was ridiculous. Sophie bet anything Persia had made it up. Her real name was probably Becky.

Sophie felt like dust, swept into the corner of her father's world. "What about me?" she whispered.

Daniel nodded. He had thought of this. He was proud that he had thought of this. "You and your mother will have to find a small apartment at a reasonable rent."

A small apartment at a reasonable rent?

They were to go from a mansion with a spy tower into some two-bedroom with a kitchenette? From a four-car garage to a slot in a parking lot? From three acres of lawn and a landscaping service to crabgrass growing in the cracks of the sidewalk?

Wait.

He was taking Persia to Egypt? Only last year, when she was her most pyramidiot, Dad had told

Mother that Egypt was too far, too expensive and too dangerous.

"I'll support you," her father said vaguely. "Don't worry, Soph."

Support. That oh-so-cruel word of divorce, meaning: Who pays for this kid now, anyway? Does it have to be me?

Sophie's spinal-tap headache exploded, gripping every brain cell. "You mean, *you're* not going to worry. *You're* going on trains and ships and planes. Whatever happens here won't be *your* worry."

They did not cringe. They actually smiled, pleased that she grasped the situation.

It was a waste of energy to spray rage at them. It had as much effect as spraying whipped cream on an attack dog.

This girl, thought Sophie, this girl barely older than my sister, will be my father's second wife. Persia Olivette. Mrs. Daniel Olivette.

"Sophie, honey," said her father, "what is there to worry about? You and your sister are grown up; you'll be fine. Edith is never going to be grown up, and I'm sorry and all that, but I have a life to live."

Sophie was sixteen. It was not grown up. Only minutes ago she had been three or four. Sixteen still needed a mother and a father. Sixteen still needed supervision and supper and a snuggle now and then.

So love *was* blind. Had no eyes. Saw no results. Considered no disasters.

"I really want your help with the wedding, Sophie," said Persia. "Love at first sight deserves an extra-special celebration."

"I want to know why there isn't such a thing as Family Responsibility at first sight," Sophie snapped. "Remembering My Original Wedding Vows at first sight."

Now she had gone too far. Her father noticed her at last and didn't care for it. He took Persia's hand and they moved toward the tower.

For a terrible moment Sophie Olivette did not believe in love. Whatever her father might claim, true love did not exist, or he would still love his wife.

But if love did not exist, then maybe nobody would ever love Sophie and maybe she would never love back.

She felt vacant and horrified. If she could not love and be loved, the whole of life was a wasteland.

Sophie blundered out of the fern room and made it to the regular kitchen, the one with the toaster and the microwave and the open bag of potato chips. Like her father, she was a fan of kitchens and glad to live in a house with two of them. But now the room made her quiver. How cold the appliances; how slick. Like Dad, they would take on a new family and remember nothing of the girls who had been teenagers here.

She wasn't going to throw a brick at her father. She was going to weep. She might as well do it on the phone with Marley. The sisters could not get along for ten minutes in person, but on the phone they could be buddies for hours.

Sophie dragged up to her room, bringing the potato chips. Salt and grease were always good company.

Jem was sitting cross-legged on the bed, plaiting Ash's long hair into complex interlocked braids. Ash was reading *Seventeen Magazine* as she got her hair done.

Sophie could not believe it. Jem and Ash had stayed? This was private. This was so private it had no parallel. Thoughtful people would have bailed out and gone home. How was she supposed to sob or call Marley now?

"Don't get too worked up about it, Sophie," said Ash. "Your mother will get a lawyer, the lawyer will drag everything out, everything will have to be divided up, they'll fight, and before you know it, Persia will be bored and back at college and your dad's affair will be over."

Could that happen? Could it dissolve like Jell-O crystals and be something else by morning?

"Forget forty-five-year-olds having midlife crises," said Jem. "Look at this gorgeous velvet dress. I want it."

"Where would you wear it?" asked Ash.

"A formal party. New Year's Eve, maybe."

So Ash and Jem had not been worrying that Sophie was downstairs slaughtering family members, but had been leafing through the fall fashion issue of *Seventeen,* picking out gowns. Persia was

Sophie's worry. A small apartment with a reasonable rent, and a mother who did not even know that this was her future—those worries belonged to Sophie. Ash and Jem had bigger, better worries.

"Hmmmm," said Ash. "Ten or twelve weeks till New Year's Eve. You could go ahead and order the gown and then hope you round up a fabulous boy to match."

Ten or twelve weeks in which Sophie's father would get a divorce, sell a house, marry a gold digger and leave for Paris.

If you thought of those weeks as school, filled with class and assignments, friends and enemies, sports and dance, they were a long stretch. But if you thought of those weeks as the end of a world, they were brief.

"I don't think we have boys like that in our high school," said Jem.

"I don't think we have parties like that either," said Ash.

Sophie felt as betrayed by her girlfriends as she did by her father. How could they talk about parties at a time like this? She should send them over to the tower to discuss weddings with Persia.

From her college dorm, Marley liked to telephone Dad and yell as loudly as she could that She Would Not Return to That House if That Person Was Still There.

Great, thought Sophie. That Person is going to marry Dad, and I'll be stuck here without my sister. But *with* my two best friends, who are not going back to their own houses where they belong and toward whom I no longer feel friendly. "I'd better hunt down my mother," she said.

"We'll go with you," said Jem.

"No," said Sophie. Bad enough they had witnessed her father. Sophie could not let them see her mother, too. Edith Olivette had gone to pay homage to some standing stones under a setting sun.

She did not yet know that the sun was setting on the Olivette family.

Chapter 3

Mrs. Olivette stared across the field and clasped her hands to her heart. "I didn't know this existed!" she cried.

Ted Larkman was in school with Mrs. Olivette's daughter Sophie. It embarrassed him to think of running into Sophie now that he knew her mother was a nutcase. "Yeah," he said. "Well. It does."

In the distance, the earth sloped up, forming a great grass doughnut in the meadow. Inside the circle, thrust into the ground like spears, were four immense upright rocks.

"This meadow has always been sacred, hasn't it?" whispered Sophie's mother. She pounced on stalks of grass like a fox on a mouse. "I can feel its past. How thrilling! An ancient stone circle right here! A Stonehenge. Is it Native American? Is it Viking?" She fastened her grass bouquet to her hat and danced a little.

Ted was not romantic. People who owned gravel pits were practical. They dealt with the bottoms of things; with heavy equipment and dusty noisy results. "Nah, it's my grandfather's," he said. "Granddad got fascinated by ancient stone circles when he was stationed in England and decided to build one of his own."

Her face crumpled and her shoulders sagged. But she rallied. "The sculptured hill, though. Such a mound was surely created one basket of soil at a time, as primitive people carried their offerings—"

"Bulldozer," said Ted. "Two days."

Mrs. Olivette did not give up. "Your grandfather felt the sacredness at this site, though, Ted. It's very intense."

"Nah. Granddad didn't care about sacred. The point was to move boulders without machinery. How did primitive people do it? How'd they drag huge rocks great distances? How many men did it take?"

Mrs. Olivette was not interested in engineering. "May I go up close?" she whispered. "May I touch?"

"Sure."

They walked together. Tall grass, golden and crunchy in the fading autumn light, brushed against Ted's jeans. Mrs. Olivette was wearing a long velvet skirt, which attracted every thorn, seed puff and briar. A navy-blue beret perched on the twist of her graying hair, and her fire-engine-red eyeglass frames were wide and startling. "Why are there only four stones?" she asked.

"If the circle had been finished, it would have had ten stones and be sixty feet across." Ted pointed to a huge gray stone, shot with glittering mica. "That was the first stone. Granddad harnessed a bunch of Boy Scouts to that one and they dragged it up from the quarry. I think he made up a badge, lied about how it was Outdoor Skills. Now for moving a second stone up there, he didn't want to use the same technique. He wanted an ox team instead of humans, but any farmer with oxen thought he was crazy and said no."

"I've always felt a deep connection with the megalithic peoples," confided Mrs. Olivette. "The Ancients possessed wisdom we have lost. We are submerged by competition, electromagnetic fields, emissions and capitalism."

Ted said nothing. But he pointed across the meadow to a rarely used dirt lane up which Mrs. Olivette had driven. (Trespassed, actually.) Sitting on the two ruts that petered out in the grass was a Land Rover.

Mrs. Olivette looked ashamed. "I like my Land Rover."

"The Ancients would have too," he comforted her. "And definitely Granddad. At first he was going to use the same tools as megalithic people. You know, dig the hole for the boulder with antlers. He antlered for about an hour. Then he said, 'Where's my backhoe?'"

Mrs. Olivette laughed. She swooped her hands

through the air as if to commune with spirits. She was in fact standing above a spirit who might commune.

Granddad had died at home, the year Ted was eleven. A doctor was there, an old poker buddy who knew the plan. A coffin was purchased and slid into the back of Granddad's smallest red dump truck (people who owned gravel pits had graduated sizes of dump trucks) and the coffin was buried in the church cemetery with a flag folded over it and a trumpet playing taps.

The coffin, however, contained a long thin stone and a lot of Styrofoam.

What they really did was wrap Granddad in a blanket, backhoe him a hole in the center of his stone circle and tuck him in. Ted didn't tell Mrs. Olivette because it wasn't legal. You couldn't just start a burying ground in your backyard, even if your backyard was a hundred and ninety acres and you felt like it.

Lifting her velvet skirt, Mrs. Olivette began dancing in and out of the stones, even the ones that weren't there. She was dancing on Granddad's grave.

"The second stone," Ted told her, "was a boulder Granddad trucked in from the woods." Of course, Granddad could have trucked it the rest of the way up to the circle, but that wasn't the point. The point was muscle power. "So when he couldn't get an ox team, he decided to roll it on top of logs, but fifteen tons is a lot of weight and he had to give up. That stone never did get into the circle."

The abandoned stone still lay in the midst of the tracks that ran around the zones of the gravel pit. The trucks drove around her and the men put up with her. She was mottled black and white, crannied with crevices and ledges and weathered smooth, the way sandpaper was smooth, not the way glass was smooth.

Now Mrs. Olivette was making offerings of gold autumn leaves to each stone. Including the stones that were not there.

Ted pointed to a straight-sided stone. "Granddad quarried that one, which isn't half as big, and made his crew move it on logs. A few years later he finally got oxen, and the mossy stone is the one *they* moved. So that was three stones, and Granddad lost interest. My dad put in that round, Santa Claus–looking one a few years ago when it had to be moved off a construction site, and Dad thought it had personality."

The stone had been too large to balance on the loader. Dad got mad at the stone for not balancing and mad at the loader for not being up to the job. Ted and his mother picnicked at a safe distance and yelled suggestions. Dad always said they were darn lucky they still had a marriage after that weekend.

"So there are four stones in the circle," Ted finished, "and one still lying in the gravel pit. Old Number Five, we call it, although it would have been second if Granddad's plans had worked."

Everybody felt affection for Old Number Five. The crew sat on it to have a sandwich and a Coke, or plopped their toddlers on top for a photograph at Daddy's job site. The first thing Dad said when he acquired a much larger loader was, "*That* could move Old Number Five."

Old Number Five was why Ted was up in the meadow this evening.

The safety inspector had announced that that rock in the middle of gravel pit traffic was a hazard and should be blasted to smithereens.

Ted knew smithereens well. At a gravel pit, that's what you did: turned rocks into pebbles. Staring at Old Number Five through the hanging dust of stone crushing, Ted knew he did not want her blown to smithereens. So he'd hiked up here to decide whether to be the third generation in the Larkman family to put a stone in the circle.

"Who bulldozed the mound?" Sophie's mother asked.

"It's called a henge. When I was little and my big brothers were in high school and their college bills were coming up, there was a recession. Nobody was building. Nobody needed sand or gravel. Dad was afraid he might lose the business. He entertained himself by surveying and bulldozing the henge. Mom was ticked. She couldn't believe he wasn't pumping gas or bagging groceries to earn a few dollars instead of moving dirt around in some dumb field."

"It's not a dumb field!" cried Sophie's mother.

"The henge is beauty and art. The stones are truth and ancient science."

Ted smiled. To his surprise, he was warming to Mrs. Olivette. There was something sweet about the way she wished things were. So he confided in her. "Nah. It was just two guys in my family with nothing better to do. Know what, Mrs. Olivette? It's my turn. I want to move Old Number Five. I think she belongs in her circle."

Mrs. Olivette caught her breath. "Yes, Ted! She *is* a female stone. And she *does* belong. Where will she stand, Ted? Here? Here?" Mrs. Olivette darted among possible stone locations.

Poor old Sophie. Ted liked her but had always stayed clear, in case she turned out like her sister, Marley: tough as a tractor. Now he saw it could be worse. She could turn out like her mother.

The future didn't look good for Soph.

"December twenty-first, the winter solstice, must be her date!" cried Mrs. Olivette. "Shall we place her in line, blending with her companions? Or at a distance, high and lonely, like a priestess in the cold dawn?"

Nobody but Ted was moving Old Number Five. Certainly no middle-aged nutcase woman was going to be in on it. Ted pulled out his father's tone of voice. The one like gravel. "I haven't decided," he said. "And as for the day I pick, Old Number Five's a stone. She's not gonna notice."

Mrs. Olivette flung her head back to gaze upon the first stars of the evening. Ted looked too. Yup. Stars.

"Oh, Ted!" she cried. "On the solstice, among these sacred stones!—within this watchful henge!—a new world rises!"

Uh-oh, thought Ted.

"I must hurry home," said Edith Olivette, blowing a kiss to Ted and dancing toward her Land Rover, "and share the joy."

———∿∿∿———

Sophie's mother was the stuff prime time is made of.

Edith Olivette knew how to set a scene. You didn't pick your vegetable garden in which to be dramatic, or the car wash, or the grocery parking lot.

You found a Stonehenge, that eerie circle of silhouettes against the sun. Perfect for camera work.

But Sophie didn't want prime time, or mid-afternoon, or any other kind of exposure. She wanted an ordinary life, with parents who remembered to have milk in the house and give her a hug and stay married.

But that is not what soap operas are made of.

Chapter 4

Because Mother would take no action, Dad and Persia were out scouting for small apartments at a reasonable rent. Sophie hoped they would fall down the stairs at one of these and travel into their New Lives in coffins.

She could just picture Daniel and Persia going through an apartment.

Oh, good, Persia would say, spiders in the laundry room. Just right for an ex-wife.

Oh, look, Dad would say, they forgot to put closets in the bedroom. That's all right, Edith and Sophie won't be able to afford clothes anyway.

Sophie had finished up the day's sobbing (it seemed part of the schedule now, like breakfast or lunch) and was methodically sorting through her childhood, looking for clues. Where had the Olivette family gone wrong?

Technically speaking, Sophie was on the

phone. Marley was calling from college, Mother had picked up her extension, and Sophie was supposed to be adding useful thoughts from her bedroom. But Sophie had set the phone down to prevent inner-ear damage.

"Mother!" screamed Marley. "Is this true? You're not even fighting? You're letting Dad get away with this? You're giving in to every demand he's making?"

In fact, Dad had made no demands. He could not be bothered—it was only his wife. He mentioned things in passing, like "The house will be sold," and then went out in his new car with Persia.

The Olivettes had always had big cars: a Volvo wagon they'd owned ever since Sophie could remember, and Mother's Land Rover, which they got a few years ago to replace a stodgy van. Ten days after he met Persia, Dad bought a tiny fast glittering Z3.

If he had bought a Corvette, he would have been in love with the engine. But the BMW was a car for when you were in love with the passenger.

"What's the matter with you, Mother?" yelled Marley. "Don't you have any spine?"

Years ago the Olivettes had had a small house on a quiet street, next door to Jem. At the old house, Sophie and Marley shared a bedroom. They did nothing but bicker. If they took a break from bickering, they were probably stalking each other. If Sophie had been nicer and Marley had been quieter, would the marriage have been sturdier?

"You cannot let Persia get a thing, Mother!" yelled Marley. "You have to get the house."

Mother said gently that Life Was Not About Houses.

Well, the Olivettes' life had sure been about houses.

Dad had had a hobby shop—model trains and planes—in a terrific location, at the best intersection. People who hadn't considered glueing together a World War II plane in their entire lives would see Dad's sign and feel the need. Then a movie megaplex wanted the site, because along with the corner came ten acres of trash land Dad had almost forgotten about. The movie people offered so much money that Dad did not have to have a hobby shop, or any other shop, or anything at all, if he didn't want to.

He didn't.

They sold the little house next door to Jem and built the wonderful house that turned up in magazines. Mom stopped teaching kindergarten, and her passions, which had been squeezed between projects for five-year-olds, had room to be full-time.

They had so much room now. But the Olivettes did not do very well with all that room. They retreated into their own corners or, in Dad's case, built more. They had their own televisions and their own computers; they had their own desks and radios and telephone lines.

Eventually they no longer had their own family.

"Marley, darling," said Mother with a certain pride, "I cannot get involved."

"What does that mean?" demanded Sophie's sister. "That's what a parent is, Mother. A person who is involved. How dare you say to your own daughter that you cannot get involved? You made me with your body. You are involved!"

Go, Marl, thought Sophie.

But Mother was not listening. The extent to which Mother heard nothing was becoming hideously clear.

Sophie opened a keepsake box in which Mother had kept their childhood art: finger paintings; early, brown Thanksgiving turkey efforts; hot mats made of Popsicle sticks.

When the house was sold, would there be a sale? The kind where you put price tags on the things you loved and stuck them on the lawn? And strangers fingered them and decided they weren't worth anything?

"If Your Father has found Another True Love in his Life," said Mother, throwing capital letters in front of words, "I must Accept that."

"Persia isn't a true love," snapped Marley. "She's just there. Kick her out. Do something. Do anything. Get a lawyer. Color your hair."

"Marley, if I am to maintain my inner harmony, I cannot get into fights or courtrooms. I have my Self and that is Enough."

In a way, it probably was Enough.

Mother had once had a spectacular wardrobe, and no doubt it would last for years in various combinations. She entertained her Self with meditation and herbal tea. It wasn't as if she had to buy a movie ticket and a large popcorn to get through the evening.

Yesterday, Dad had told Sophie cheerfully to think of herself as having two families now! Wasn't that lovely?

"What do you think this is?" Sophie said to him. "A multiplication problem? You think my friends who haven't had the privilege of watching their parents divorce are whining about it? Demanding a second family of their very own?"

"Aw, Soph," said her father, "will you just try to see my side?"

"No," said Sophie. "You don't have a side."

On the phone, Marley's voice cracked. Was she exhausted or giving up hope? "You guys aren't even divorced yet. Nobody's even filed. And you want to know something, Mother? The Parent Formerly Known as Dad—"

Except for the *v* in *divorce,* that was the saddest phrase Sophie had ever heard.

"—told Sophie and me to call Persia our stepmother."

The minute Sophie was threatened with a stepmother, she found that the world was knee deep in them; they were everywhere, growing like weeds, coming up in cracks in the driveway, taking over houses like crawling vines. Word spread through high school about Sophie's future, and it turned out that in every class and on every bus somebody had a stepmother.

And it turned out that some stepmothers were nice and some stepmothers were loved, but nobody claimed that the second family measured up to the first.

"I will never refer to Persia as a stepmother," announced Marley. "I will refer to her as roadkill."

"Please think harmonious thoughts, Marley," said their mother.

"Harmony?" yelled Marley. "Mother, have you lost your entire mind or just pieces of it?"

The doorbell rang.

Sophie had never been so grateful to abandon a situation. She bounded out of her room and down the hall.

The front foyer rose two and half stories, with a vast chandelier, sheets of window, and a floor of black-and-white marble. Sophie whirled down the curving stairs. It must be Jem or Ash.

Her girlfriends were more concerned about what they'd wear to a New Year's Eve party to which they had not yet been invited than about Sophie's problems. "How's it going?" Jem would ask sympathetically, and before Sophie had time to answer, Ash would jump in. "Yesterday we went to three more stores. Nobody is carrying that dress we saw in the ad."

Sophie resolved that today she would say nothing about the divorce, would laugh just as much as Jem and Ash, would even think in terms of boys and dating.

But Persia got to the front door first.

In some weird way, Sophie kept forgetting Persia. The whole thing was so impossible. Sophie was shocked all over again to see this slender golden thing darting around the house as if she lived here. It was certainly better to have Persia out hunting for a hut for Sophie to occupy than to have her inside this very house, touching doorknobs.

"Brandi!" cried Persia, hugging a girl Sophie had never seen. "I'm so glad you got here. There's so much to talk about."

Brandi was stunning. Her outfit looked as if she had bought it five minutes ago and would never wear it again, but shop tonight for something even trendier.

Brandi hugged Persia back. "You look beautiful. True love becomes you."

Sophie wanted to say, "She's roadkill, Brandi," but she could not get the words out. Brandi and Persia were friends. There was something sacred about friendship, especially friendship inside her own home, and Sophie could not kick it in the shins and call it names.

"Brandi, this is Sophie," said Persia, pasting an uncertain smile on her face.

It was evident that the name Sophie meant nothing to Brandi. Persia had skipped the part about her one true love having teenage daughters.

Persia's pretending too, thought Sophie. She's pretending Daniel Olivette is single and childless. And it's going to work for her, because once they're abroad, there will be no trace of a previous family.

"Love your shoes, Sophie," said Brandi. "I tried those on, but they didn't fit me."

Sophie approved of excellent shoppers. Was it possible that she was going to like Persia's friends? Or were the shoes contaminated now and she should spray them with Lysol and even get some in Persia's eyes?

"Well!" said Persia. "Let me show you the house."

They walked in line: father's future trophy wife, trophy wife's friend and—last—the daughter.

"Marvelous house," said Brandi. "Lovely colors. Although I'm having a great time at college, Persia. Do you really want to start doing laundry and fixing lunch?"

"I won't be doing laundry," Persia assured her. "And we're not going to live here. We're going abroad. I told you how much we want adventure."

Sophie hoped terrorism would be on the rise while Persia was in Egypt. A few masked men with submachine guns were the adventure she deserved.

"How is Daniel?" said Brandi, in a guarded voice that interested Sophie.

"Daniel's turning forty-five," said Persia. "It's a crisis for him, and he has not acknowledged it."

I'd say he's acknowledging it, thought Sophie. He's marrying you. If that isn't a crisis, I don't know what is.

"Oh, Persia!" said Brandi. "I can't be polite for another minute. I'm so worried about you. I understand falling in love. I was in love last year. But Daniel's *old,* Persia. I agree he's handsome, I loved when we all had dinner, and he was such a gentleman. But it was like sitting around with somebody's father. He's—" Brandi threw courtesy away. "Let's be honest here, Persia. He's just an old geek. His hair is white. You can't marry him."

It had not occurred to Brandi that Sophie might be related to the old geek. Brandi was probably imagining a stepcat, or a stephamster, but not a step—

—*child,* thought Sophie. Dad and Persia could have *children*!

Sophie was very sorry she had thought of this.

"I love him," said Persia, with a certain dignity. "Now, this is the spy tower. Come on up and see the view. Are you going to be able to be a bridesmaid? The ceremony will definitely be on New Year's Eve. Isn't that romantic? He'll carry me over the threshold into a new year and a new marriage."

"What if he has a heart attack lifting you?" said Brandi. "And besides, what about the guy's wife?"

Well, good, thought Sophie. At least somebody admits the guy is married.

Sophie took one step on the tower stairs and could not go on. It was too much the territory of Persia and the Parent Formerly Known as Dad.

"Daniel is in superb health," snapped Persia. "He works out constantly. You would never dream that he's in his forties."

"I would dream it," said Brandi, "and it would give me nightmares."

Terrific, thought Sophie. Brandi and I are

going to end up best friends, sitting in the back-seat while Dad and Persia drive.

Persia said stiffly, "As far as the first marriage goes, it's just paperwork. Then she's history."

Sophie stumbled toward her own room. A room of your own has one unbeatable asset: a door. Sophie opened her door with nothing in mind but closing it.

Mother was there, bouncing on Sophie's bed. "Sophie, darling," she said eagerly, "I want to introduce you to the circle."

In the olden days, there had been knitting circles and sewing circles. But the Mother About to Become History was referring to a stone circle.

"I suppose I could see what the fuss is all about," said Sophie reluctantly. I don't get to fuss, she thought. I'm supposed to say, Oh, goody. Divorce. Oh, goody. A stepmother. Oh, goody. A small apartment.

"Sophie, it isn't fuss! It's the perfection of earthen circles under the dome of sacred sky."

Sophie uttered a tiny prayer that her mother was not talking like this around Ted Larkman.

—◦◦◦◦◦◦—

A soap opera has to have lots of yelling.

This was Marley's role.

A soap opera has to have dense people, who never catch on.

That would be Mother.

A soap opera has to have lots of selfish people.

That would be everybody else.

A soap opera does not need anybody nice.

That would be Sophie. Opinion not needed.

Chapter 5

Ted was the only person in high school whose future was known to him.

He would do what his father had done, and his grandfather before him. He would run the gravel pit.

Everybody else was faced with a hundred thousand choices: from hamburger slinger to computer analyst; from cruise-ship staff to poet. Everybody else had to search his heart and mind and hands, constantly on the lookout for clues: little pointers to the field he or she would choose.

Ted was the only kid in school who would skip that.

He knew.

He'd always known.

When he looked at Mrs. Olivette, still trying to find her place in life, struggling and whirling and hoping for clues, he felt like the luckiest guy on earth.

There were kids in school like Mrs. Olivette. Frantic kids. Kids who thought they might like medical school, or else underwater archaeology. Kids who wanted to film wild animals in Africa, unless they decided to become stockbrokers. Kids who were fiercely determined to get the highest grades and scores and be ready for any door that opened, and were on every committee and in every group, their eyes continually shaded to figure out their own personal horizon.

Most people pulled it off. Wherever they were going, they got there. But some, like Mrs. Olivette, got their gears stuck in neutral. They could only spin.

Used to be, Ted could count on being alone in the meadow except for the deer at dusk. But now Edith Olivette was here constantly—trotting toward him—calling, "Yoo-hoo, Ted!"

Last week she had decided that she could no longer drive up. This being a sacred site, the proper approach was on foot. Today, for the first time, she had Sophie with her.

Ted never worried about what to say to Mrs. Olivette. She could carry on a conversation with or without another person. But what he was going to say to Sophie? She looked as lost as an orphan.

Ted had never considered marriage in his life, not anybody's marriage, ever, but now he considered two of them: the Olivettes' (dead in the water, half of it circling stones) and his parents' (solid as bedrock). He had never thought of himself as a person involved with marriage. But now he could see that marriage was crucial; it was the center of the world. Your parents' marriage, whether it existed or not, would always be the most important marriage in the world.

"Ted!" cried Mrs. Olivette. "You knew we would be here, didn't you, Ted? You felt my need."

No. Ted had felt the need to make Old Number Five plans.

"I," said Edith Olivette, with that short word making it clear who mattered, "have had a difficult, difficult day, Ted."

Ted figured Sophie's day hadn't been so hot either. He smiled in her direction.

"Hello, Ted," said Sophie. Her clothing seemed stronger than she was. Denim jeans held up her legs, wool jacket kept her body attached, baseball cap fastened down her hair.

"Hi, Soph." He was working out a more complete answer when Mrs. Olivette began skipping along the top of the henge, picking milkweed pods and puffing little milkweed stars into the air. How would Sophie react when her mother began dancing among the stones? Especially the stones that were not there? Mrs. Olivette was careful to avoid these. Ted was used to it, but Mrs. Olivette was not his own personal mother. Ted doubted if you got used to that kind of thing in your own mother.

"Ted!" cried Mrs. Olivette. "I can feel the earth

move! It's speaking to me through my feet! It's humming!"

He almost let that pass. But he couldn't quite do it. "Nah. That's the quarry. They're blasting."

The blast made him think of his dad, which made him think of home, which brought him back to his parents' marriage. Sickeningly, it occurred to Ted that he didn't actually know anything about their marriage. It wasn't something he paid attention to, any more than he paid attention to the electric bill. What if the Larkman marriage was not bedrock, but rocky?

Ted's throat felt dry. Time to head home, grab a soda, check out his parents' marriage. "Why don't you come on down to the house right now?" he shouted over to Edith. "It'll be a good time to ask for permission. My folks are home." The sentence jarred him. Sophie's folks were never going to be home again.

"Permission to do what?" said Sophie.

Mrs. Olivette wanted to dance here by moonlight, and that was a problem. Ted's parents were not going to let somebody wander around their very dangerous property in the dark.

Ted didn't answer Sophie, because he didn't know where to start. But he came from a long line of men who never said a thing, and it suited him.

She didn't ask again.

Marley Olivette glared at the young doctor at the clinic. "What do you mean, I'm not sick?" she snapped. She had no use for medical types who disagreed with her diagnosis.

"Ms. Olivette, you do have a sore throat. But you have no fever, no sign of infection, and you've just admitted that you spend an hour every day screaming at your parents." He paused. "An hour? That's a lot of screaming."

Marley noticed that he was a very good-looking doctor.

He became stern. "I'm not prescribing antibiotics, Ms. Olivette. I'm going to suggest you stop screaming."

Marley closed her eyes. "I will tell you what my father has done. Then see if you think any daughter could do anything but scream."

The doctor said, "I really cannot stay to hear this. I have a waiting room full of patients."

"They're not sick either," said Marley. "Listen to my story."

●━━╲╱╲╱╲━━●

Sophie tried to emulate Ted and say nothing and show nothing. It was an old swamp Yankee trick, and Ted was born to it, but Sophie was not, and what she really wanted to do was lie down and bawl.

She almost flung herself into Ted Larkman's care. He was solid and rectangular, like the standing stone that had been hacked out of the quarry.

She reminded herself that they never even spoke at school, hadn't spoken since about fourth grade, and the purpose of this invitation to his house was to get Mother permission to do something that would undoubtedly upset Sophie even more than she had been upset ten minutes ago.

If she walked down to the Larkmans', she would have to walk back up here, and then all the way home, and Sophie was so exhausted by her family she didn't want to go anywhere unless she could be carried. Perhaps Ted would carry her. He certainly looked strong enough. He looked as if he routinely ran around carrying cement blocks, instead of moving them on a forklift.

They were on the top of a hundred-foot cliff out of which great blocks of stone had once been blasted. Water had filled the old quarry and lay dark and deep, out of reach of the sun. A chain-link fence close to the dropoff seemed no more useful than netting. "Ted," said Sophie, "I could roll up that fence and take it with me as I fall to my death."

He laughed and shifted her to the safe inside of the path, while he walked on the fence side. The weight of his hands on her shoulders was comforting. If only he would keep his arm around her. But his attention was already elsewhere. "There's Larkman Gravel," he said, pointing. She studied his face for a moment before following his gaze.

Below lay mountains of gravel, vast orange

machinery for crushing, and two bright yellow bulldozers, blades lifted as if ready for dinner.

Ted owns this world, thought Sophie, staring at Ted's profile, and it owns him. Soon Mother will own nothing. What am I going to do if my mother really is a pyramidiot and I'm left alone with her, because Marley won't come home and Dad flies away?

She found that she was holding Ted's hand. Hanging on was such relief. But she knew she must not do it. She must not require of anybody that they turn into parents, or support. Still, she didn't let go. She wanted to take Ted home with her, or at least his hand. His was as big and rough-surfaced as a cement block.

The lane forked, and they turned away from the gravel pits, circled a small hill covered with oaks, and arrived at the back steps of Ted's house. Sophie let go of Ted, and he held the door for them.

It opened into a slop room for peeling off filthy clothing and hanging up hard hats. Sophie's father would hate a room like this; Daniel Olivette liked order and beauty and style. Mother had discarded those . . . but Persia had them all.

I was wrong that the marriage went down as fast as a computer crashing, she thought. It's been going down for years, and I didn't notice.

The Larkman kitchen was dull and brown, with plain white appliances and a big old table. Daniel wouldn't think much of this, either. He'd spent months comparing faucets from Italy and fixtures from Sweden.

Mrs. Larkman, chubby in a pink sweatsuit, was reading a paperback in one hand and stirring something on the stove with the other. "Oh, hi," she said as if Sophie and Edith trooped into her kitchen all the time. "Have a seat." She shoved mail and newspapers out of the way, lifted laundry off chairs, opened a box of Oreos, and tossed it across the table. "So what's up, Edith?"

Sophie had to sit there while her mother spoke of moonrise and how it stirred her soul, how it opened channels through the cosmos and led Edith into spiritual harmony.

"I know in my heart," said Sophie's mother, "that in the dark, the standing stones speak to one another in their own tongue. I must be present. I must participate."

Ted's mother nodded expressionlessly. Then she turned her back and walked sideways to fill a teakettle and put it on the burner.

Dad and Persia laughed at Mother; Jem and Ash laughed; now Mrs. Larkman was laughing. If I could laugh at Mother, would this be easier? thought Sophie.

Ted dealt each person a half dozen Oreos and held one up, silently demonstrating the Oreo cookie wrench. Then he waved his freed-up chocolate wafers, scraping the icing off with his front teeth and licking the remains. He leaned toward Sophie and said very softly, "In situations like this,

Soph, a person needs a hobby." He ate the icing-bare chocolate wafers in a single crunch and gave her a sloppy grin, lots of crinkles, as if he'd spent so much time squinting into the sun from the cab of a tractor that his face had aged a decade ahead of the rest of him.

Sophie's mother paused for breath.

Ted thrust an Oreo into her hand to occupy her. "What we need," he said, "is a good name for our circle. Some circles in Britain have names like Merry Maiden and the Stone Dancers and Whispering Knights. There are hundreds of stone circles in Europe, you know, and they all have names."

"*I* knew that, of course," said Mrs. Olivette, "but I had no idea *you* would." She looked at Ted as if it were quite remarkable that Ted had learned to walk, let alone recognize a circle.

"There's a legend about one of those circles," Mrs. Larkman said, working her way through her cookies as fast as Ted, making Sophie jealous of a family that split Oreos together. "A bride was turned to stone."

"Cool," said Sophie. "We'll get Dad and Persia up here and turn their little bloodlines to granite."

Her mother actually laughed.

Ted did not. He slammed his fist down on his Oreos, sending chocolate splinters across the table. "How come you're not fighting, Mrs. Olivette? You think those Ancients who were willing to drag some eighty-ton stone to Stonehenge weren't fighters? You have to fight Daniel! The Ancients would have stabbed and kicked and ambushed and knifed! They'd have slashed and burned and pillaged and—"

"Ted," said his mother.

He flopped back in his chair and swept smushed Oreos into his palm. "They would've," he said sullenly. "And she should too." He ate chocolate out of his hand.

Sophie wanted to kick somebody.

Mother wouldn't talk to Sophie, she wouldn't talk to Marley, she wouldn't talk to Dad and she wouldn't talk to a lawyer. But she would show up at that ridiculous stone circle and talk to Ted Larkman.

A minute ago, Sophie could have slid into a crush on Ted. Now he was just proof that Mother could get involved with anything and anybody—except her daughter.

Mrs. Larkman put her hands on Sophie's rigid angry shoulders and massaged slowly and deeply.

Don't, thought Sophie. Stop. I'll cry. Nobody has touched me in so long.

"How about your name, Edith?" said Mrs. Larkman. "The Edith Stones. I like that."

How sane and solid Mrs. Larkman was, in her sane and solid kitchen, among ordinary solid brands of groceries. Sophie's mother hardly even knew what groceries were anymore. She went shopping only for Truth.

"I hate my name," said Edith grumpily. "Why wasn't I named Valentine or Christabel?"

In front of Ted, sounding like a fourth-grader writing in her diary. Sophie tried to hang on.

"Pam," Edith confessed, "I want to dance at the circle by moonlight. Pam, I have come to understand the importance of the sun in finding inner peace. I want to celebrate the solstice this year, among my friends. Might I invite them to the stone circle for Solstice?"

Sophie felt a desperate anguish. How could Mother find anything to celebrate right now, let alone the number of minutes per day that the sun shone? How could she place her faith in a row of rocks instead of an attorney?

Ted's mother quit massaging. She flung herself backward against the wall, like a paper doll. She stared at Edith.

This is it, thought Sophie. This is when the neighbor says, I'm taking command here. Call an ambulance. This woman needs intensive care.

Sophie picked up the last Oreo so she'd have something to eat in the waiting room.

Eventually every soap opera ends up in the emergency room.

Sophie was in favor of this ending because it would mean that real grown-ups, grown-ups who understood trauma, would take over.

But Sophie was not the scriptwriter.

Her parents had chosen the sets, the props, the budget and the supporting cast.

Sophie was more like the invalid in the hospital bed whose remote had dropped to the floor and who was stuck helplessly watching a channel she hated. She couldn't even mute the sound or turn her head.

Chapter 6

Marley knew that she bore the responsibility for what had happened between Daniel and Persia.

During those few short days in which she and Persia had been roommates, Marley had spilled her guts. "My mother," Marley had said, and she was off and running, listing her mother's flaws.

"Your poor father!" Persia exclaimed.

"Can you imagine living with her?" Marley agreed. "I'd be out of there in a heartbeat if I were Dad."

It was girl talk. Dorm talk. It had inside it the slovenly cruel way in which many wives referred to their husbands and many kids spoke of their parents. It was a copy of the least pleasant talk shows, where the whole purpose was to say ugly things about somebody you formerly loved.

But for Marley, as for anybody who tuned in

to those, it was entertainment. This was how you talked: you threw your family around. It didn't mean anything.

Persia, however, took Marley seriously. Daniel Olivette was in need of rescue, and who better to rescue him than Persia herself? When Persia came home with Marley that weekend, Marley abandoned her, racing off to see real friends. It never crossed Marley's mind that her roommate and her father would bake bread together and, by dawn, discuss a future together.

Marley did not want to have any idea why Persia would want such a thing. She just wanted it all to go away. And yet she could not stop herself from lifting the phone and screaming, and then screaming some more. The sole result of Marley's strategy was a sore throat.

The doctor said, "Ms. Olivette, if you want to prevent that marriage, you'll have to go home and handle this in person."

"If I handled it in person," said Marley, "I'd have a knife in my hand."

To her surprise, he began laughing. Now she saw that he wore no wedding ring. Marley could move as quickly as Persia (although Persia had not cared about the wedding ring situation). "Let's have dinner," she said to him.

"You mean—a date?"

"You were too busy in medical school ever to have one of those?"

"Well, no. No, I have had dates. Just not—well—not—"

"Not with girls who give themselves sore throats by shrieking at their own father," said Marley.

"Right."

"I promise not to scream. What's your name, anyway?"

"Dr. Hawkins."

Marley loved flirting. She had been good at it since eighth grade, when she looked up one day and found that all those gross little boys had turned into delightful not so little boys. "I'm supposed to call you Doctor? You know my blood pressure. I should know your first name."

"Joe," he said, smiling.

Handsome. Smart. Older. A doctor.

Sold, thought Marley Olivette. "Joe the doctor. I like it." She gave Joe her world-class smile.

It was not love at first sight. It was simply that this man was husband material. Of course, if anything developed, Marley would *say* it had been love at first sight. She intended to have a romantic engagement whether it was romantic or not.

She might have lost the edge on her speaking voice. But she had not lost her smile. Joe the doctor said, "Okay. Yes. Dinner."

Got one, thought Marley Olivette, already planning their engagement and how many children they should have.

Had Persia said that? she thought next. *I've got one!* It didn't matter if he was the right age. It didn't matter if he was earning a living. It sure didn't matter if he was single. Persia got one. It doesn't matter who you get. Get anyone. As long as you have one.

———◆〜〜〜◆———

In the Larkman kitchen Ted's mother clapped her hands and *she* began dancing.

Ted and Sophie looked at each other.

"Edith! You are brilliant!" cried Pam Larkman. "That is the answer! New Year's Eve is also our thirtieth anniversary, so I need a really special place for our party. But I left it too late. Everything is booked. I thought our party was ruined. Edith, you had the answer all along. It's that stone harmony, it's given you wisdom. We'll dance in the stones. We'll rent a tent. We'll have a great band." Mrs. Larkman ate her final Oreo with a decisive chomp.

Thirty years of marriage, thought Sophie. My parents hit twenty-one and threw in the towel. I wonder when a marriage is safe forever. Thirty sounds safe. Would a person wake up in the morning after three whole decades and decide this wasn't such a great idea after all? No. The Larkmans are safe.

Pam Larkman grinned wickedly at Edith. "And Porta Potties!" she added. "We'll put them right in the stone circle. We've got six spots just waiting for something tall. Talk about body harmony!"

Sophie laughed hard enough to tip over. As long as she was falling over, she might as well fall against Ted. Yup. Solid as a quarry wall.

Edith said faintly, "Let's not put the Porta Potties into the stone circle."

"Mom was kidding, Mrs. Olivette," Ted reassured her.

"No, I wasn't," said Mrs. Larkman. She yelled, "John Larkman!"

"Uh-oh," Ted muttered to Sophie. "She uses both Dad's names, Dad's in trouble." Ted shifted his arm and brought it down on Sophie's shoulder. Sophie thought she might have a crush on him after all. We have Oreo cookie breath, she thought. That would make a nice first kiss.

"John Larkman," said Mrs. Larkman when he walked into the room. "New Year's Eve is solved."

John Larkman was short, stocky and weathered. He was beyond tanned and into jagged and split and squinty, like his rocks. His hands were harder than work gloves and his calluses were stones themselves. He had little patience. He was often rude. He had no use for most people. He preferred gravel. Mr. Larkman didn't waste time being polite or even speaking. Sophie was afraid of him.

"New Year's Eve has been having problems?" he said.

"Our party. Wait till you hear what Edith and I planned."

Sophie's mother flapped around like a heron with red glasses. "First, please, John. Promise me the solstice."

Sophie put her Oreo back on the table. Edith was serious. This silly date mattered to her. Her marriage didn't matter. Her shelter, income and food didn't matter. Her daughter didn't matter.

But the solstice and the stones—they mattered.

Dad's right, thought Sophie. How could I expect him to go on living with her?

How would she have felt if Dad had just moved out and there had been no Persia? What was it that really upset Sophie? The end of one marriage—or the beginning of another?

"Solstices are free," said John Larkman.

"She means at the circle, Dad," said Ted.

"It's not a circle, unless you guys have been real busy."

"But it's *meant* to be a circle," said Edith desperately. "I can feel the circle there."

I won't cry, Sophie said to herself. I've lost my sister to college, and my father to Persia, and my mother to this woman Edith. But I won't cry.

John Larkman's hard blue eyes in their tight squint assessed Edith. Then he said softly, "I agree. The circle is there, waiting for its stones."

Sophie's mother trembled. "And the solstice?"

"It's yours, Edith."

"The circle is there?" Ted said to his father when he had driven Sophie and Edith home, and gotten back, and set the table for dinner. "Waiting for its stones?"

John Larkman grinned at his son and cuffed

him lightly. They weren't men who hugged; they wrestled. "The woman's husband left her for a college girl, Ted. She feels better believing there's a circle in the meadow, give her the circle."

"Dad, she needs more than a stone."

"She needs a job," said Dad. "She caught on yet that Daniel is gone in eight weeks? She's on her own?"

Ted did not know. He had wanted to stabilize Edith on the drive home and make friends with Sophie. But he hadn't thought of anything to say.

"And what are you doing for New Year's Eve, Theodore?" said his mother.

"Huh? I thought I had to help with the sound system and lighting for your party."

"You do. I'm asking if you're bringing a date." His mother's eyes shifted slowly and meaningfully to the chair where Sophie had been sitting. "Your brothers," his mother informed him, "had girlfriends from the time they were in seventh grade."

Ted hardly knew his brothers. They were ten and eleven years older than he was. They were men with wives and toddlers, and they showed up at Christmas and for a week in the summer. They phoned now and then, and Dad would say to Ted, "Want to talk to Chris?" and Ted would say, "Hi, Chris, how ya doin'?" and Chris would say, "How's school?" and that was it. Same time next year they'd say it again. Who cared what they did in seventh grade?

"Teddy," said his mother.

He hated being addressed as Teddy.

"It's a major event." She spoke carefully, as if he were the densest of her three sons, the one for whom things had to be pronounced clearly, in order to penetrate his thick skull. "You'll want to share your parents' thirtieth anniversary with somebody special," she enunciated.

Ted's first date was certainly not going to be the anniversary of his parents' marriage. Asking a girl to celebrate marriage with him? That was one serious calendar notation for a person you didn't even know if you were going to keep liking her.

But he was happy. A party after thirty years sounded like a good marriage. He studied his father. He could not, in his wildest dreams, imagine asking Dad to discuss love and marriage. "I," said Ted, "will not have a date. I will be too busy filming you guys dancing around Porta Potties."

•—₩₩₩—•

It was a soap opera, so one party was not enough. There couldn't simply be some little Solstice gathering—a few peculiar middle-aged women smiling into the sun.

No, it had to be a great splash of an event, soon to be followed (on the same set; how thrifty of the sponsors) by a New Year's Eve party, which itself was a thirtieth-anniversary party.

And then of course, a wedding.

What a wardrobe opportunity.

Edith Olivette was not a star in clothing and accessories. Luckily Persia and Daniel could take up the slack. Ted and his parents did not understand clothing and would have to be kept offstage as much as possible.

But Sophie loved clothes. She loved fashion and she loved shopping.

Exactly how was she to shop for parties that celebrated the end of the last year in which she possessed a family?

Chapter 7

Saturdays were like little boxes. They didn't flow into each other the way Monday through Friday did. You had to open a Saturday separately and make special plans for it. Sophie sat on the top step of the stairs thinking of possibilities.

"Soph!' yelled her father from his brick ovens. "Come talk to me? Please?"

Up wafted the warm, everything's-okay smell of baking. Sophie found herself running into the French kitchen, where the fragrance of bread could have softened the hardest heart.

When Dad baked, he liked to spend hours—with mixing bowls, open cookbooks, apple cores and measuring spoons on every surface. The kitchen was wonderfully messy. He rolled up a scrap of dough, whisked it around the board to gather sugar, and handed it to Sophie. He smelled of bread and cinnamon, and she loved him so completely that not one thing he had ever said or done mattered at all.

Dad rolled up a second raw dough treat. Sophie was opening her mouth like a little bird when Dad dropped it into Persia's. Sophie had not even seen Persia, who was tucked into a brick corner, perfect as a magazine illustration. Her hair was twisted in romantic golden curls. "Hi, Sophie," said Persia. "Isn't this fun? Don't you love this? It's all homey and cozy. I never had this before. I didn't have a homey home." Persia patted the countertop next to her; a sit-by-me pat; a let's-be-friends pat.

But it was Persia who *stopped* the house from being homey. Persia was splitting this family as casually as Ted and Sophie had split Oreos.

Sophie's father was looking at her so hopefully. This was the gift he wanted; his daughter's friendship with his future wife. He wanted Sophie to exchange her mother for Persia, like exchanging shoes that didn't fit.

"Soph," said her father, "I thought we'd all drive up and visit Marley. We're starting to make plans for the actual wedding, and of course we want you and Marley to be involved. We should start thinking about gowns and hairstyling appointments."

We, thought Sophie.

Her father was still a pair. He hadn't gone one day without a partner. For him divorce would not be a separation. He wouldn't ever be separated. But for her mother, that terrible, going-two-ways *v* in *divorce* would last a long time.

"Daniel didn't even realize," said Persia, giggling in a girlfriend way, "that you had to schedule the hair appointments earlier than the wedding."

All my life I'll have to listen to her call my father Daniel. As if she knows him.

I still say this isn't possible. I cannot be sitting in my own kitchen with a girl practically my own age who wants to talk about her marriage to my father.

"See how I have my hair?" said Persia. "I think the three of us should do our hair just the same. Mine is gold, Marley's midnight black, yours burns red like a sunset."

Sophie stifled the urge to rush to a mirror and admire herself, burning red like a sunset. Persia, you skunk, she thought. You're trying to seduce me, too.

"We're going to be beautiful," said Persia. "I can hardly wait."

The Parent Formerly Known as Mother wants us to be accepting, thought Sophie. This is the moment. My future stepmother is telling me how beautiful we three happy girls will be. But I don't want to be there when Dad promises for a second time to love a woman for better or for worse. It isn't a promise you can make more than once.

And quite suddenly, Sophie hated her father.

It was pure hate.

It was not diluted by any circumstance.

It was hate.

He had taken away any hope of true love. If Sophie ever did fall in love, she would be suspicious. Her father had taught her this: There is no such thing as lasting love. There is only love while it is convenient.

Persia said, "Sophie, go coax Edith to come. We'll drive up together to visit Marley."

Sophie imagined this. Dad and Persia in the front seat. Mother and Sophie in the back. Friendly conversation about divorce. Joyous plans for second weddings. Marley being a peach.

For a tottering, sickening moment, Sophie thought her mother might be right. Planets and moons were crashing through the universe, forcing love on this person and ripping it out of the heart of another. You were a molecule thrust in space, hoping, hoping, hoping for love.

Persia was hoping to be loved, not just by Daniel. *By the rest of them.* Persia wanted Sophie's love and Marley's love and even Edith's love.

"Is Marley expecting us?" Sophie asked.

"She's expecting *me*," said Dad. "I told her we need to talk about finances and her next semester."

"Are you going to pay for her next semester?"

"Already did," said Dad. "This is just an excuse to go see her. I miss Marley. And I really want you and Marley and Persia to be friends."

Friends had to be ordinary. They had to be a plain old part of the day. If she became friends with Persia—went shopping with Persia—had hair appointments with Persia—it might not betray Mother, who approved of harmony, but it would betray the family. Sophie wanted her same old family a lot more than she wanted harmony. So she said, "Mother isn't home."

"Where is she, do you know? We could pick her up," said Dad, as if they were discussing some high-school game—hot dogs and bleachers and extra sweatshirts.

Mother was up at the circle, planning her Solstice party, deciding how many candles she needed. She was happy the way a four-year-old can be happy, absorbed in the moment. Any day now Sophie was going to find herself calling Mother in for her nap.

"Oh, well, let's just us go," said Persia. "Is the picnic hamper ready, Daniel?" She beamed at Sophie. "I've always wanted one of those wicker baskets filled with yellow china and cotton napkins, and you take them on your picnic and you sit in the grass and everybody envies you. So Daniel bought me one."

Sophie sat alone in the middle of the Volvo wagon with her seat belt for company. Dad and Persia sat in front, and the back was filled with cardboard boxes and the picnic basket. For Dad, the Volvo was just an old car he'd driven a million times. For Persia, it was just boring, no style or romance.

But for Sophie, it was the family car in which they piled skis and down jackets for weekends in winter, and towels and beach chairs for weekends in summer. The one that carried Sophie and Marley on long-ago Halloweens when it poured and they didn't want their costumes wet. Like that rainy year Sophie had been a tyrannosaurus and Mother had painstakingly sewed red potholders into triangles for the dinosaur spine. And what about the time Sophie broke her arm, and sat in that very front seat between her two parents as they drove way too fast to the emergency room?

Who was going to remember all this when the family broke up? Not Mother. She wasn't involved. Not Dad. He didn't even know anything was breaking.

Sophie tried to picture their arrival on the college campus, where Persia had been a student for so few days. What was Marley going to do when the three of them piled out of the car, the way families got out of cars?

Sophie was glad she had a big sister who could be counted on. No matter what, no matter who, Marley was never going to be a peach.

"I found a buyer for the house, did I tell you?" asked her father.

She could feel her heart diminish and cramp and stop sending blood to her brain.

A buyer.

Somebody like Persia, with no memories. The rooms would just be space. No echo of fight or affection, of celebration or sorrow.

I have no home, thought Sophie. "Dad, please don't sell. Let Mother and me stay in the house."

He shook his head. "It's the only way Persia

and I can afford the year of travel and still buy a cool house when we get back."

"And which half of the house sale goes to Mother?" said Sophie.

"Edith doesn't want it. Anyway, most of the money was payment for those ten acres, and they were never Edith's. It's going to be such a relief not to be chained to that woman."

You weren't chained to a woman, Daddy, thought Sophie. You were married to my mother. You still are.

He and Persia kissed at each red light.

Sophie threw herself back against the seat and let the belt snap around her. It was one thing to see your mother and father kiss. It was allowed. They could even go and make babies if they wanted, like you. But this! Yuck and vomit.

"Now, Soph," said her father briskly, "get Edith to go see that apartment I rented. You have to decide which furniture you're taking."

"Dad, Mother is not ready. You need to give her more time."

"She's out of time!" snapped Daniel. "Today is November twenty-second. In four weeks, the moving van is coming. I scheduled it for December twenty-first."

"But that's the solstice," protested Sophie. "Mother's party! You know how important that is to her."

He shrugged. "It was the only day that worked for me. My schedule is tight."

He was down to one pronoun. *He* mattered.

His schedule. But *us,* the family, thought Sophie, there is no such word left in his vocabulary.

Sophie could not stand the sight of their heads, Persia's cheery bouncing hair and her father's beginning bald spot. She turned so far around that she was looking into the way back of the wagon. She frowned. "What's in all those boxes?"

"They're for packing my stuff in," said Persia. "I never emptied my half of our dorm room. I've got a ton of stuff to collect. All my best CDs. I hope Marley didn't let anybody borrow them."

Why were diplomats struggling to bring peace to the world? People who were fighting felt like fighting, and they enjoyed fighting, and they weren't going to quit fighting until they were good and ready. Sophie was not good and ready. Forget harmony. She was going to throw bricks and smash windows. "You're not driving up to the college because you miss Marley," she said to her father. "You're going to get Persia's stuff. Stop the car, Dad."

It wasn't so much that her father obeyed as that they were at a corner and the light was turning yellow anyway. Sophie could not sit another mile with those two. She jumped out of the car and slammed the door. Pity their fingers weren't caught in it. She stomped away from the car, as if grinding her feet into the earth would keep her from calling her father names. Then she stormed toward home.

Dad put the Volvo into reverse and tried to catch her.

Sophie crossed the road by putting up her hand and stepping out. The driver of the next car didn't want blood all over his finish, so he shrieked to a stop and she reached the far side alive.

In the Volvo, her father shrugged. He turned his back. He drove on.

So something had been killed, whether or not the blood spatter showed.

Her family.

Eventually, on a soap opera, somebody is bound to run away and vanish.

The cast could go on without Sophie. Edith and Daniel and Persia could have all the episodes they wanted.

People could tune in anytime and wouldn't have lost the thread of the story. Every now and then somebody would say, "Wasn't there this adorable young daughter at one point? What happened to her, anyway?"

But what Sophie wanted was to go home and have it be home, *and have the soap opera vanish instead.*

Chapter 8

"Well, well, well," said Marley. "The Parent Formerly Known as Dad."

"Marley, we just want to be friends," said Persia. "We want you to understand."

"Get a life," said Marley. "I might have a splinter of respect for you, Dad, if you were giving the house to Mother, but you're dropping her like some old head of lettuce into the garbage."

Although, in fact, Mother looked like an old head of lettuce. Once she had been fashionable, the only mother Marley ever met who wore hats, and in them looked triumphant and strong. Now she treated her body like a post, tacking signs onto it and forgetting to take them off after it rained.

"Why can't you be happy for me, Marley?" said her father tiredly. "Try to understand. Your mother was off on a retreat to strengthen her Self, because God forbid she should strengthen *us*, and into my home comes this beautiful woman who says, 'Daniel! You have this marvelous French kitchen and you've never been to France? Wouldn't you love to sit at a sidewalk café in Paris? Stay in a castle where a princess lived? Walk the ramparts of a medieval city?' "

"So why didn't you wait till Mother came home," said Marley, "and take *her* to France?"

Dad made his you're-missing-the-point face.

"Daniel and I have brought a picnic, Marley," said Persia. She listed the menu, like a waitress mentioning specials. Or a future stepmother hoping to become special.

I hate this, thought Marley. I hate this so much I don't know what to do with all my hate.

They were in front of Marley's dorm, where rusty red chrysanthemums circled around benches and little trees. Marley knew quite a few of the students soaking up the late-November sun. She hoped nobody would come over. She would be forced to introduce her father and his future wife.

Of course, anybody who knew Marley also knew who these two people had to be. She had spent the last two months shrieking the news to any available listener. She was suddenly more humiliated by her own behavior than by her father's. "What are you two doing here, anyway?" she demanded. "You know perfectly well I'm not going to have a picnic with you."

"My reason is that I want you to be in our wedding," said Persia.

Marley dreamed of weddings as much as the

next girl. But not my father's! she thought. "I hope you have a better reason, Dad," she said grimly. She was shocked by his expression. I went too far, she thought. I didn't know you could go too far with your own father.

"I came to talk finances," he said quietly. "I paid for your second semester. And don't worry, I'll pay for your next three years, too."

"What about Persia?" demanded Marley. "Don't you think she should finish college before she gets married? Is this the example you want me to follow? Dropping out?"

Although Marley and Persia had had the usual introductory talks in their room and Persia had mentioned family, Marley had not listened. When other people talked, Marley used the time to plan what to say when it was her turn again. If her turn didn't come fast enough, she just interrupted. Now it occurred to Marley that Persia must also possess parents.

"What do Persia's mother and father think about this, Dad?" said Marley.

He actually blushed.

"He's older than my parents," said Persia in a low voice. "They're a little antsy about the whole thing. But I'll bring them around. I'm their only child, they have no choice."

"Oh, Dad!" Marley found her fingers yanking at her hair to give herself bald spots, a horrifying habit she had had as a toddler. She unpeeled her fingers and crossed her arms in front of her chest where she could keep an eye on them. "Dad," she said, and her voice broke along with her heart. "How are we ever going to get together as a family?" The word became dear again, and so did the other three members of her tiny little family.

"What about Thanksgiving, Dad? It's only five days away. We can't give thanks for our family. Not with this divorce sitting next to us. And no other Thanksgiving will work either. You've messed up too much. You're ruining our family, Daddy, and you're probably ruining hers." Marley's horror ate into her voice and turned it into a whisper. "You can't do this. It isn't right. It isn't fair."

"I'm sick of being fair. I've gone out of my way to be fair. As far as Thanksgiving goes, you need to come home and do your packing, so the stuff you want to keep gets shipped to the apartment."

Her father was a total stranger. She had not the slightest sense of ever having met him. She didn't have much sense of knowing herself, either. "Dad," she said, "do something generous for Mother. Whether she asks for it or not." Although Marley had not been generous with her mother for one second.

"Please, Daddy," she said to her father. "You don't have to pay for my next three years of college. I can get loans. But give Mother half the house. She can't get loans."

It took Sophie forever to walk home. By the time she could see Dad's tower down the block, her feet hurt more than her heart. Being human was such a pathetic undertaking. No sooner did you stomp off to ponder the meaning of life and marriage than the only thing that mattered was your baby toe.

Ash and Jem turned into the drive just as Sophie did, almost mowing her down. Ash had a little turquoise-blue pickup truck she was very proud of. She liked to shift with much flexing of muscle, as if taking a semi up a steep grade. "Where've you been?" asked Jem, flinging open her door.

"Out. What are you guys up to?"

"Driving around. Want pizza?"

Sophie could not stand the thought of food. She wasn't sure about company, either. "I have a lot to do. I'm going to look at my clothes and decide what I can bring to the apartment and what I have to take to the thrift shop."

"Oh, goody!" cried Ash happily. "Can we help?"

"She doesn't mean 'Oh, goody, your life is ending and you even have to throw out half your sweaters,'" said Jem quickly. "She just likes anything about clothes."

"Great," said Sophie, although it was not. "Come on up."

Ash opened the closets. "Your wardrobe will fill the entire apartment," Ash informed her. "You'll have to live in the park in a sleeping bag and hope policemen are kind."

"And how's your mother?" Jem threw in courteously.

"She's busy hating her name. She doesn't want to be Edith."

"She doesn't like *her* name?" snorted Jem. "She should try mine. My parents thought there were too many Jessicas and Jennifers so they'd set the style with Jemima. It's way worse than Edith."

Sophie was so tired she could hardly tell a shirt from a sweater, never mind make choices. Her thoughts swirled like white chocolate into dark. She bet Dad wouldn't have shrugged if Persia had gotten out of the car miles from home.

"You know, Sophie," said Ash sternly, "you're running out of time. You're the only person in the family sane enough to stop things. If Persia gets the house money, she'll spend it in a year, and then what do you bet she dumps Daniel?"

Sophie felt disconnected and floaty.

"Here's what your family will be if you don't stop this house sale," said Ash. "Nuts and broke."

Sophie's feet still hurt. She sat on the bed.

"Your only hope," Ash went on, "is not to have a house to sell."

"What do you mean?" asked Jem.

"If there's no house," explained Ash, "there can't be a sale of the house. Persia gets nothing. And she'll bail. Soph! How happy you will be! Without a house, there will be no divorce, no stepmother, no small apartment."

"Bulldoze the place, Sophie," said Jem, and giggled.

Sophie felt hot and strange. She had looked down upon a huge yellow bulldozer very recently. Two of them, actually.

She imagined the great steel blade lifting

from the ground. The huge metal tracks rolling inexorably toward the mansion. She heard the smash of bricks and glass as bulldozer rammed tower. She saw the entire roof lying on grass, splintered by chimney and stair. In her bulldozer, Sophie would crush into rubble those plans for Traveling with a New Wife to a New Life. Persia would be screaming amid the broken glass, her beautiful face twisted with greed and frustration, and then she'd stalk away, because all she ever wanted was the money. Dad would beg for forgiveness, pleading with Sophie to let him come back into the family.

Sophie, high in the driver's seat in her yellow hard hat, would look down and sneer. Then she'd run her steel treads over his Z3.

Ash and Jem were looking at her uneasily.

Sophie managed a slightly sane smile. Inside, she was not sane at all. She was zapping streaks of lightning and giddy wild laughter. Bulldoze the house! Of course. Why hadn't she thought of that?

"We're kidding," said Ash. "If you really bulldozed your house, you really would be nuts and broke."

"Anyway," said Jem, "you don't have a bulldozer."

"That's true," said Sophie.

But I know who does.

It was only right that a soap opera should have some destruction.

Building was fine in its place, but demolition was better.

What a character to introduce.

A bulldozer. Yellow. Stylish. Strong. A mind of its own.

So how furious am I? thought Sophie Olivette. Furious enough to bulldoze my house to stop this? I'd be the envy of every single child of divorce. ("You guys wanna split? Wait till you see what I'm gonna split in return.")

For the first time, Sophie had the power to write the script.

Chapter 9

"**Y**ou be secretary," said Ted's mother the following afternoon. She handed him a pencil and a stiff-backed notebook.

Huh? Secretary? What was that supposed to mean? Ted squinted at his mother.

"Ted, close your fingers around the notebook or it will fall to the floor." Pam Larkman pointed to the other stuff he was to carry and then said, "March. We'll get this done tonight, it's the only night I have."

Ted's box was extremely heavy. He saw in amazement that it was full of sand. "Sand?" he moaned. "Mom! How come we're not driving? It's a quarter mile to the stones. We have a whole row of trucks with full gas tanks. I'm *carrying* sand when we could—"

"Edith wants as little as possible to do with motors. We're celebrating nature, not engines."

"Mom," said Ted.

"I don't want to spend an evening yelling at my youngest child," said his mother, "so take notes and don't whine. John Larkman," she went on, "you're carrying the candles, the paper bags and the flashlights."

Dad shouldered his cardboard box.

Edith and his mother set off, chattering happily and carrying nothing.

"I should never have been polite to Mrs. Olivette that first day in the meadow," Ted muttered to his father. "I should have said, 'No. You can't touch. Go home.' She'll never go home now."

His father grinned.

"Dad, would you please put up a fight about carrying this stuff?"

"In this marriage," said his father, "your mother makes all holiday decisions. Even holidays I didn't know about, like Solstice." Dad shifted his box. Candles bumped waxily against each other. "Living with another person isn't a picnic, Ted. You spend most of your time agreeing to something you don't care about, don't want and can't understand."

Ted was not heartened by this view of marriage. "Then why do it?"

They walked uphill. Gravel crunched. Leaves drifted.

To Ted's infinite surprise, his father answered, "Love."

Sophie knew better than to stop and think about the bulldozer plan.

It was the kind of thing where if you thought about it even for ten minutes, you'd know you were pathetic and hopeless and needed to be tranquillized. So thinking was out. Action was in. The instant Ash and Jem were gone, she changed into nice comfy sneakers and tore across town toward the quarry.

All this exercise was beginning to pall. She needed to be more like Marley, and place demands. Make sure Dad gave her a car of her own before he vanished into Persia's clutches. On the other hand, how many people start by driving a bulldozer? Sophie would definitely be the first on her block.

She could just barely make out the path into the woods that led to Ted's property. When she darted in, trees closed around her and tentacles of bittersweet and poison ivy clutched her clothing. Any other night, Sophie would have fled screaming. Now she hardly noticed. Women who were going to bulldoze houses were not afraid of spiderwebs in the dark.

She broke out of the woods into the high waving grass of the meadow. The sky was painted gray and black. The first few stars seemed to stoop down and take an interest. Sophie waved and they twinkled back.

She had to stop running because the frozen grass was so slippery. She could have worn two ski jackets and not gotten the hollow between her shoulders warm. The silence of the dark field was solid and impenetrable.

A light appeared between the grass and the sky.

It was not attached to anything. It had no source.

She remembered her mother's claim that the standing stones awoke in the night and spoke in their own language.

The henge lunged at her out of the dark.

"Here," Edith was saying to Ted's mother. "This is a magical spot."

His father sighed. "I hate sitting on grass," he said to Ted. "Edith, of course, is opposed to plastic chairs. I'm going to bring up hay bales for people to sit on. That should meet the nature requirement. Listen to her, going on about which stone is magic. It would be magic if she'd get a job and pay attention to her kid."

Mrs. Olivette had spent more time designing the cutouts in the luminarias than on Sophie. Ted could not imagine what it must be like to have such unparent parents.

Ted's parents were always there, and if they were not home, they were still there, because their rules and requirements, habits and tastes littered the house; the house was knee deep in all that the Larkmans were and had been.

Sophie and her mother had not yet gone to

look at the apartment, but Ted had driven by. It was a large complex of two-story buildings. No grass, just parking lots. He'd driven around to see if the apartment had a backyard, because Ted could not imagine a life without land, but there was just more parking.

What had Mr. Olivette said when he signed the lease? "Oh, this is just right for my little Sophie. A view of the Dumpster for breakfast. Well, off to Paris."

Of course, if Sophie had been a different kind of person, she'd have been thrilled. These were a mother and father who would never know if she did drugs, dropped out of high school or hitchhiked to Florida.

"Dad," he said, watching the mystery that was Edith Olivette, "do you think any particular stone is magical?"

"If they had magic, Ted, would they let me blow 'em up and crush 'em down into pea gravel?"

—₩₩—

Sophie was suspended in horror.

The four stones inside the henge were moving. *They walked.* The stones *were* frozen people, and at night they *did* speak in their own tongues, and—

Sophie stomped her foot, slipped on the icy grass and slid down the mound as if on a snowboard. She was too mad to fall. "You're all nuts!"

she yelled. "You're just encouraging her. What are you guys doing up here, anyway? You might as well open a Dunkin' Donuts, it's so crowded."

"We're just experimenting, Sophie," said Pam Larkman. "There are details to work out."

"You couldn't use flashlights like normal people?"

"People who build their own Stonehenges aren't normal," said Ted. He was laughing. His candle flame gave his face a chiseled look, as if he came from the stones.

"Hello, darling," said her mother happily. "We're trying to figure out if our guests will break their ankles if we have nothing up here but candlelight."

"It depends who you're inviting," said Sophie, trembling from fury and embarrassment. "If it's the crystal-gazers and the angel freaks, they probably don't even know how to turn a flashlight *on*, so you might as well use candles. Of course, you'll want to hire a resident grown-up to strike the match."

John Larkman chuckled like friendly gravel. "Sophie," he said, saluting her with his candle, "you're growing on me."

I'm falling in love with Ted's family, she thought. I can't let myself do that. It's bad enough I'm daydreaming I can stop my father's plans with a bulldozer. I can't daydream that I'll be a Larkman in the morning.

"I wish we could have confetti," her mother

said forlornly. "But we must not litter. We'll use birdseed."

Our lives are dissolving and she's worried about whether confetti will dissolve. *Grow up!* Sophie wanted to scream. A solstice isn't a holiday, it's hardly even a mark on a calendar. Can you please pay attention to things that matter?

A terrible desire to be mean engulfed Sophie. Parents were so catching. They were like flu. Stand around them, breathe deeply and you'd be doing what they were doing. Picking the solstice for moving day was just being mean.

But Sophie, too, could be mean, and it was certainly her turn.

I'll tell Mother now, she thought. Now, when she has an audience and can't hide, the way I couldn't hide when Dad told about his second marriage in front of Ash and Jem. I'll say, There is no party, you pyramidiot. You'll never have a party again and it's your own choice, you gave away everything.

"Go ahead, Edith, use confetti," said Pam Larkman. "Anybody complains, we'll whip 'em."

Sophie let herself into a daydream in which she had Pam Larkman for a mother. This moved into a closely related daydream in which she had Pam Larkman for a mother-in-law.

"Sophie," said Ted, unzipping his jacket with a loud rasp, "you didn't even wear a sweater. Wear this." He was already putting his jacket on her. It was like being zipped into a teddy bear.

"Oh, that's wonderful," she said. "Thank you, Ted. But are you going to be warm enough?"

He didn't bother to answer that. Boys were always sure they were warm enough. In a just-between-us voice, he said, "Soph? Are you okay? I mean, we *expect* Edith to come darting out of the trees, but you were kind of a surprise. Has something else happened?"

Mother had not noticed how odd it was that Sophie had popped up, with or without warm clothing. Dad had not called the house to see if she'd gotten home all right. They had ceased to worry about her. Worry is a component of love, so when nobody is worried about you, perhaps you are not loved. Sophie fought tears and the desire to love this person who had put something warm around her and taken her hand.

"What do you think ancient stone circles were really for, John?" said Edith.

"Lots of theories," said Ted's father. "Sacrificial altar. Cattle pen. Eclipse predictor. Cult of the dead. I don't think there's any mystery, though. People just need to leave a mark on the world."

Ted astonished Sophie by whirling her around, giving her a fierce hug, and then another. "Look at that sky!" he said, and he actually lifted her from the waist, holding her up toward the stars like the strong man on a cheerleading squad. "A whole world out there, Sophie. Waiting for you and me to make marks on it."

He laughed and set her down. The moment vanished, and there was no indication that the three parents had even noticed. There was not even an indication that Ted himself had noticed, because it was Sophie's mother to whom he spoke next.

"Mrs. Olivette, you know how in England not all standing stones are in groups. Sometimes there are solitary stones. Well, moving Old Number Five into the circle is a problem. We bring a truck and a backhoe and a fifteen-ton stone up here, the ground is wrecked. Better to have grass for our parties than mud and ruts. So why don't we put Old Number Five *outside* the henge? Face her toward the sun or the moon, whichever you think is right."

"All by itself, Edith, the stone would look so proud," said Mrs. Larkman. "Independent."

"Not just part of a circle," said Mr. Larkman.

They had rehearsed this. Edith Olivette was their five-year-old. They were offering her a lollipop. Sophie wanted to scream: *Just keep her. She's yours.*

Edith shook her head. "When I taught kindergarten, I learned that every child wants to be part of the circle. No child wants to be on the outside. Children on the outside aren't proud. They aren't independent. They're lonely and sad."

"Well," said Ted, "that's kindergarten. But we're talking rocks here, Mrs. Olivette, and Old Number Five isn't going to be lonely or sad wherever we stick her. She's a rock."

Back when Edith Olivette cared about fashion, she'd had a scarlet wool coat and a great bright scarf with fringe that fell to the ground. With her lovely dark hair and a great crazy plate of a hat, she looked smashing. These days she mostly looked crushed. But now she drew herself up in the shivering candelight and was beautiful again. "Getting Old Number Five into the circle matters more than grass. And I stand by my dates. She must be in the circle by December twenty-first." Edith Olivette blew out her candle and extended her right hand.

Pam Larkman sighed, blew out her candle and took Edith's hand.

Ted put his hand on top of theirs.

Mr. Larkman folded his arms safely over his chest.

There's nothing scarier than pyramidiots making a deal, thought Sophie. "Ted," she said, "is it true we're standing on top of your grandfather?"

———•—∧∧∧—•———

There aren't many children in soap operas.

People don't want to watch children get hurt, and hurting people is part of soap operas.

I'm being too grown-up, thought Sophie. If I were behaving like a child, people would comfort me.

Chapter 10

Ted could only half look at Sophie. The memory of lifting her was intense and disturbing. Ted didn't do things like that. Girls interested him in a remote way, not a lift-in-your-arms way.

Sophie wearing his jacket had confused him, he decided. At least he knew now why guys gave girls their team sweatshirts. It was possession without effort and without touch. He didn't want the jacket back. He wanted to think of the soft fleece lining against Sophie.

"Yes," said Ted. "It's true."

Wind whipped across the rim of the henge, rattling dead leaves and sifting dry grass. Their candles went out in a row, each little flame vanishing behind the curtain of night.

"Buried here?" said Edith. "But I went to his funeral and stood at the grave. I remember how you covered your face with a handkerchief, Pam, you were crying so hard when they lowered the coffin."

"I was laughing," said Ted's mother.

"You were not," said Edith.

"I couldn't help it. It was hysteria."

Ted relit his candle. Sophie touched her candlewick against his, and when her flame shot up, he felt a funny little collapse inside him. He had trouble seeing around her. She filled the entire spread of his gaze.

Mrs. Olivette thrust forward her candle to be lit too. Ted knew why Daniel Olivette would leave his wife. It would be easy to leave her—and hard to stay.

And yet. And yet.

What was this thing called marriage, where some people said, Okay, fine, I'll carry the luminarias uphill instead of using the truck? And some people said, No, I'm going to Paris. You get an apartment with a view of a Dumpster.

"I'm still embarrassed," said Ted's mother. "The veterans put a flag on his empty grave every Memorial Day."

Ted made fingertip cups in his soft candle wax. He carved a smile into his little wax puppet and poked two eyes. Then he peeled away the tiny doll and gave it to Sophie. She smiled as if she had been hoping and hoping for a wax fingertip doll. "Thank you, Teddy."

In fifth grade every girl had had a teddy-bear backpack. They snuggled and cuddled up to their backpacks, calling them little bear names; dumb names, which the boys in class then used for Ted.

Ted was hostile toward people who called him Teddy. But when Sophie said "Teddy," he felt soft and squashed.

"Exactly where is he buried?" asked Edith.

Ted pointed to the middle of the circle.

Sophie was wearing the doll on her thumb. She tucked her thumb safely into her palm, under the roof of her fingers. "Mom," she said, "you've danced on his grave."

Mrs. Olivette was delighted. "I think that's what he wanted. A little dancing on the grave. A little laughter under the moon." She took John Larkman's right hand and Pam Larkman's left. "This," she said, "calls for celebration. There *is* a spirit here, and we knew him well. Let's dance."

Ted was deeply impressed when his father obeyed. Mrs. Olivette can do anything, he thought. So why doesn't she?

Sophie's eyes were shining. "Shall we dance, Teddy?"

Ted did not know how she was doing it, but Sophie was getting prettier every time he looked at her. Now Sophie was—well, pretty wasn't the word. More—well—beautiful.

But dance with her? Ted remembered hideous elementary-school square dancing, as he tried to get in and out of a swing, holding sweaty hands with other desperate people. And Sophie really was a dancer. He had seen her in those tights they wore. "I can hop, Sophie. That's my only dance ability."

"The key," said Sophie, "is to hop on alternate feet." She took his hand.

This was their third hand-holding. Ted was feeling pretty secure about holding hands now. At this rate, he'd probably have sex for the first time when he was thirty.

"I'm usually driving a truck," he told her. "I need four wheels to keep my balance. Two feet aren't enough."

"But since I also have two feet," said Sophie, "we do have four."

Ted's parents were waltzing. Ted was stunned.

Edith had spun out alone to the far side of the henge. They could see just her candle, as if her body had departed, leaving only one flickering trace of the woman herself.

"She's wearing me down, Ted," said Sophie. "I don't have a whole lot of balance left. And it's hardly begun. I haven't gotten her to pack. I can't even get her to visit the apartment."

It began to snow, quickly and without preliminaries. No little snow scouts came down first to see what the weather was like. The whole cloud emptied out. Sophie was starred with snowflakes. Would she want to keep his jacket? Would he want her to?

"I feel pretty balanced," he said to Sophie. "I'll be your other two feet."

●━━\/\/\/━━●

"Come on," said Pam Larkman. "Let's have dinner. I have a casserole in the oven. Probably charred by now, but let's see what we can retrieve."

The three grown-ups walked downhill. The two

teenagers followed silently. He'll be my other two feet, thought Sophie. What did he mean by that?

I'll be her other two feet, thought Ted. What did I mean by that?

"I've found the musicians for my party," said her mother. "A recorder, a lute and a tambourine."

"That is not music," said John Larkman. "That is squeaking and plucking."

Sophie had to smile.

Squeaking and plucking is what I've been doing for weeks, she thought. My father is abandoning us, and I'm letting *him* decide the day it happens? What's the matter with me? I am perfectly capable of telephoning the moving-van people and choosing a better date than December twenty-first. So what if it doesn't fit Dad's plans? The whole point is that I don't *want* to fit into Dad's plans. I want—

Sophie remembered the bulldozer.

—•—/\/\/\—•—

They ate in the kitchen, where the centerpiece consisted of unread newspapers, unopened junk mail, and a pile of gleaming chestnuts.

This was a house that had never been decorated to start with, let alone redecorated. On the wall were family photographs and a last year's calendar illustrated with race cars.

Parents should be like Ted's parents: working at the same job, living in the same house, using the same old calendar, and most of all, married to the same person.

Mrs. Larkman even cooked the same recipe she'd probably cooked for thirty years—macaroni and cheese casserole with crushed potato chip topping.

John Larkman bowed his head and offered a blessing, and Sophie *was* thankful, but also jealous. How come *she* didn't get to have all these blessings? How come the world was packed with happy families and not one of them was hers?

———— -\/\/\/- ————

Ted had a third helping of macaroni, carefully cutting the potato-chip crust to give himself extra topping. Mom didn't cook much during the week because she was too tired from work, but weekends they had real meals, like this. He loved real meals. He loved company at real meals. He looked happily at Mrs. Olivette and Sophie. Company was good.

And then, wonderfully, his mother slid dessert out of the oven. She had made apple crisp from the sharply sweet Macoun apples in the old orchard. Ted jumped up to get plates and vanilla ice cream.

"You know, Mrs. O.," he said, "solstice is the day with the fewest hours of sunlight. The very next day there is *more* sunlight. So on the darkest day, you'll be facing the light."

Edith stared at the old race-car calendar. "Maybe if my husband weren't getting married again the week after the solstice," she said, starting to cry. "For me the darkest day is going to last a long time."

His mother handed two plates of apple crisp to Ted. "You and Sophie go have dessert in the TV room and let us have some peace."

Dad hated tears. He'd wave his apple crisp around, hoping to be excused from the sob session. Ted hoped Mom would stand firm and not let Dad follow them into the TV room. With any luck, this would be just one of the many things in his marriage that Dad didn't want and couldn't understand.

Ted led the way to the TV room. Sophie shut the door behind them. Ted collapsed on the couch so hard he had to lurch to keep the apple crisps on their plates. The forks shot off onto the carpet. Sophie, establishing herself as an excellent person who didn't bother with annoying sanitary details, picked them right up and shoved them into the apples again.

Ted was long and large. Once his back was against the heavy sagging pillows, his knees stuck out beyond the sofa cushions and into the room.

Sophie, however, sat on the very rim of the couch, as if the Larkmans didn't let guests have more than an inch at a time.

She had a wild, excited look about her. She pressed her lips together as if kissing and then let them fall apart as if drowning. She set her apple crisp on the floor. She pulled her knees tight together so that she became a small, beautiful package. She made a steeple from her fingers. Her wax doll was hidden inside the church of her hands. She looked straight into Ted's eyes and took a very deep breath.

She's going to propose, thought Ted.

Chapter 11

It was a proposal.

It was not for marriage.

"You want to bulldoze your house," repeated Ted.

She was bouncing on the sofa cushions now. All of her was bouncing. He disciplined himself to listen, although looking was better.

When people were excited about things, Ted liked them more. At this point he was liking Sophie enough that if he liked her any more he couldn't use the word *like*. He felt as if he were pitching off the cliff into the quarry, and all he had to hold on to was a fork and a dessert plate.

"Here's my plan," she whispered.

He loved whispers, when you were the only one allowed to hear.

"The house will be rubble," breathed Sophie. "The buyer will have nothing to buy. My father will be out of money. Persia will skip town." Her voice returned to normal. "Everybody," she explained, "will live happily ever after."

"Cool plan," said Ted. "Except where will you do your happily ever after living? You won't have a house anymore."

Sophie brushed this away. "There's insurance. We'll put it back together."

"Nope. Insurance covers accidents. It's not gonna be an accident if the daughter mows down the house with a bulldozer. There won't be any insurance."

Sophie frowned.

"You bulldoze his house and your father will hate you." Ted ticked off his fingers in front of her face. "He'll be penniless. Homeless. Marriageless. Loveless. Trip-to-France-less."

Since her dessert was on the floor at a distance, Sophie took Ted's fork and ate some of his apple crisp. She was a girl, so she actually looked around for a napkin. Ted's mother was still teaching napkin basics to Dad, never mind Ted. "And Marley can never come home," he added, "because there is no home."

Sophie had more of his apple crisp. She fed him a forkful. Suddenly there was a great deal to do: argue, eat, stay normal, breathe, look at Sophie.

"Not only will your mother end up in a rent," he said with his mouth full, "it won't even be a reasonable rent, because nobody will have any money. Your mother will end up in a rusted-out trailer. Eating boiled potatoes."

"Uh-oh," said Sophie.

"But if you bulldoze the house anyway, I'll visit you in prison," he offered. "I'll come every Thursday at five. We'll look at each other through bulletproof glass. I'll marry you in thirty years when they set you free."

"Come on. The judge won't give me thirty years."

"You'd be a threat to the community. A person who bulldozes her own house could do anything."

Sophie was thoughtful. "Let's go back to that part where you marry me in thirty years. Would you consider ten?"

"Ten what?"

"Years before you marry me. We'd be twenty-six. That's a good year for getting married."

Ted could no more imagine being twenty-six than he could imagine loaning her a bulldozer. "So the bulldozer plan is off?"

"It's modified. I won't bulldoze the entire house. I'll just take down the tower. The buyer will back off, because a pile of glass won't appeal to him. We'll still have bedrooms and bathrooms. Dad won't hate me, either, because once he sees that all Persia wants is his money, it will be a relief to know his daughter still adores him."

"What daughter still adores him?" asked Ted. "Is there a third daughter I haven't met? Not Marley? Not Sophie?"

"I will pretend to adore him," said Sophie, "and he will fall for it and come home—"

"—such as it is," said Ted. "A pile of rubble at one end of the property."

"—and we'll be the family we once were," she finished triumphantly.

Why was it Ted's job to bring Olivette women back to reality? But he could not let that pass, any more than he had let Mrs. Olivette believe that the vibration from blasting was the earth's conversation. "You're not the family you once were," he said quietly.

Sophie slowly drew away from him and slowly retrieved her own apple crisp. She studied the two desserts. She handed him the untouched dessert and stuck a fork into what was left of the other one as if intending to snap the fork in half.

I lost my chance, he thought. I should have skipped the truth. Now we have food between us, instead of—but he did not know what had been between them.

Her eyes were like Edith's, except Edith focused on some Other Thing, while Sophie focused on Ted. "I still say it's a good plan, Teddy. Just show me how to use the bulldozer."

There would be the minor matter of getting his father's permission. (Dad? I want to lend Sophie a bulldozer? No big deal, she's just going to wipe out half a million dollars of building.) Dad might waste ten seconds on this. (You don't inherit the gravel pit, Ted. You're too dumb. You can sell used toothbrushes.)

"I can show you how to use the bulldozer,

Soph, but your house is a couple miles from here. You can't drive a dozer on a road, the metal tracks chop up the surface. You have to drive it onto the flatbed and then drive the trailer to your house, which you don't have a license for, and anyway, I bet a thousand bucks you can't back a bulldozer off a flatbed trailer, and then—"

"*You* can," said Sophie. "I was never going to do this alone. You and I are going to be a team."

"How do I explain my actions to the police?"

"They'll go after me," said Sophie. "You point the bulldozer, I'll take the house down."

You did not drive a bulldozer the way you drove a regular vehicle. It had a de-accelerator, not a gas pedal, two steering columns, forward and reverse, but not like the stick shift of a car, even if Sophie had ever driven stick, which he doubted. If Sophie wrecked the gears, his father would put cement blocks around his ankles and throw him into the quarry pond.

"You have more than one bulldozer, don't you?" said Sophie. "I saw them in the yard."

He nodded. "The company has three. You saw the baby dozer and the big one—fifty tons. It's usually rented out, because not many people own one that big."

"Could it take the tower down?"

"The blade's five feet high and fourteen feet across. Solid steel. I guess it could take anything down. But Dad would never say yes." But Ted imagined it. Mr. Olivette, inside the tower with

Persia, staring at the approach of doom. When a bulldozer crawled, the blade, like a glacier, picked up everything in its path and redistributed it. The redistribution of that glass tower would be quite an event.

It occurred to Ted that there were enough people around building things. He should branch out. Smash stuff. T. Larkman: demolition expert.

"Well, then, let's not use the fifty-ton," said Sophie.

"Soph, if you saw the fifty-ton approach your house with the blade raised, you'd definitely panic. But the little dozer, see," he said, and he had to stick the dessert plate somewhere, and had to take Sophie's hand, and the effect was like cutting fuel to a diesel engine: he stalled instantly. He could not remember the topic, let alone what side he was on.

Sophie giggled softly and Ted mumbled, "See, the eight-ton, it's not gonna strike fear into the heart of your enemy. It's the kind of bulldozer where guys who rent one stand around and go, 'Awwww, that's cute.' "

"So it's the teddy bear of bulldozers?"

"You can't use it. It doesn't have a covered cab. Falling glass would kill you."

Sophie pressed his hand against her. He could feel her heart racing. It seemed to Ted that he slid off the couch into a puddle of hormones. One minute he was concerned with the stripping of gears on heavy equipment. The next minute he would have wrecked anything anywhere to strip gears with Sophie.

"How about the middle-sized bulldozer, then?" she said seriously.

"Sophie! What do you think this is? Goldilocks and the three bears? That bulldozer is too big. That bulldozer is too small." He was laughing. He was dying to do it. "Soph. It wouldn't work. And I think it would be a crime."

"It's a crime what my father is doing to my mother!" she cried.

"I agree. But it's his crime, not yours."

"Oh, Teddy," she said, starting to cry. She pulled herself away from him, tucking her knees up to her chest now, so that along with being a tiny package, she was an untouchable package. "I could see the house coming down. I could hear the crunching and breaking and snapping. I could see Dad standing in broken glass, begging for forgiveness—but you're right, Teddy. My family would be exactly what Ash said. Nuts and broke."

Ted could not stand to see tears in her eyes. He felt weak and desperate. He ordered himself not to yield on the bulldozer issue. Why couldn't he be with some normal girl who just wanted to go to a movie?

On the other hand, the world was full of normal girls. He had never wanted to take one to a movie yet.

Sophie walked over to the window. By day you could see the tops of the distant chutes and crushers. At night, the only sign of the gravel yard was a tiny Christmas tree on the top of the highest chute, twinkling through the night, all year long.

"A Christmas tree is up already?" said Sophie. "It isn't even Thanksgiving."

"It's always there," said Ted. "For luck and for blessing."

"Rock-bound John Larkman believes in the power of a sprig of green?"

"It's just a thing you do at construction sites," he said. "You see a crew building a bridge on a highway, you'll probably see a little tree at the top of their crane."

He wanted to put his hands around her again. But first he wanted to think about it. He hadn't expected to feel like this.

The door of the TV room opened.

"Yoo-hoo!" cried Edith. "Time to go home!"

•──◦◦◦─◦∿◦◦∿◦◦∿◦◦◦─•

Well, there was one person with whom Sophie could always discuss boys.

Marley.

Marley had her faults, but dislike of boys was not one. Marley believed the only really great topic was boys. The instant Mrs. Larkman dropped them off and they went inside, Sophie raced to her room and dialed Marley.

"Oh, Soph, I'm so glad you called," said her sister. "I'm dying to talk. Guess what? I'm in love.

I've met the right man. He's a god. He's mine. I hooked him. He has fallen into my arms forever."

"Did he say so?"

"No, he's very quiet. But I understand people. I know what he's thinking."

"Are you bringing him home to meet us?" asked Sophie.

"Get a life," said Marley. "I can't breathe around Dad. Dad even came up to the college today. With *Her*. Can you believe it? They wanted to Be Friends. They wanted me to Understand."

Sophie was struck dumb. That was *today*? Today she had been cozy in the kitchen with Persia? Today Dad had announced that the house was sold? Today she had leaped out of the car, stormed home, heard about bulldozers and fallen for Ted?

Impossible.

That kind of thing took weeks.

"As a matter of fact," said Marley, "we were in the center quad, a thousand students and their book bags racing by. We were sitting on a bench. I was at one end. Dad and Persia were scrunched at the other end. There was so much space between us that some guy came and sat in the middle and we had to talk over him."

Talking to Marley was always fun, which was mysterious, since she and Marley couldn't get along.

"I threatened them with tires on their spines," said Marley, "but they didn't even twitch. Soph, no, I'm not coming home. You come here instead. We'll go to parties, you'll meet cute boys. I, of course, have met the cutest one."

"I've met a pretty cute one myself," said Sophie.

"Tell me," cried Marley. "I want to know everything."

"Ted Larkman."

There was a little pause, the kind sisters know so well. Marley repeated, in the voice of one asked to remove a leech, "Ted Larkman."

Sophie saw Ted through the filter of her sister's eyes. Physically and mentally, a little too stocky. A little too solid. Back in middle school— the last time Marley'd seen him—a boy who had to think too long before he spoke.

Sophie's mother would have defended Ted. ("He just had to grow into himself; now he's a fine young man with a lot to offer.") Marley would not agree. Marley would say, "Once a dud, always a dud."

"Are you going out with him?" said Marley in a say-it's-not-so voice.

"No. I just see him around. Tell me about your boyfriend," said Sophie quickly.

Marley's voice turned smug. The older sister who had gotten there first, with the best. "He isn't a boy," she said. "He's a man. He's a doctor." Marley discussed at length the superiority of her new love.

Sophie couldn't help it. She tried to climb into the conversation with a sentence or two about Ted.

"Sophie, *please*. There is *no* comparison. Ted

is a *dork* who carries *pebbles* around in *buckets. I am dating a* doctor."

The reasons Sophie had rejoiced when Marley left for college were coming back to her.

"Okay, so Thanksgiving is Thursday," said Marley, who always took possession of the subject as if she were playing football. "Joe is going home to his parents in Wisconsin. Who would have thought anybody lived in Wisconsin? Anyway, I have to have Thanksgiving with you and Mother. What are we doing?"

Sophie could hardly bear thinking of Thanksgiving. Dad was having Thanksgiving with Persia. That most family of holidays—and he would not be home.

She was desperate to have Marley at home; Marley's energy and anger and wicked remarks here where they belonged. "When will you get here?" she asked her sister.

"I'm not driving down there," snapped Marley. "You and Mother come here."

Sophie wanted to throw herself at the Larkman family feet, shrieking, "I'll do anything! Dishes! Pots! Feeding the hogs! Just let me pretend I have a family like yours."

A doctor.

He couldn't be a postal clerk or a water-meter checker. He couldn't sell insurance or manage a Pizza Hut.

No.

This was a soap opera. He had to be a doctor. It was too bad he was just a doctor in a college clinic, but this could be remedied. He could move to the big city and specialize in brain surgery involving refugee children. Every now and then he could rescue a cocker spaniel.

When do I get an episode? thought Sophie, and then she killed the thought.

All the episodes were hers, even though she was in the audience, or backstage, or supplying props.

A family soap opera has glue at the bottom. Nobody's feet leave the stage.

Chapter 12

Tuesday night, Marley and Joe were at a basket-ball game. This was Joe's idea. Marley did not care for athletic events. She liked her men in suits and ties, trying to get possession of money and cars. She did not like them all sweaty, fighting for possession of a ball.

Joe was so absorbed by the game that Marley began to feel a little less fond of him. He had turned out to be the kind of guy who stomped and cheered and whistled with two fingers in his mouth. Shouldn't medical school crush that stuff out of you?

When Marley offered to finish school on loans if Dad would give Mother the house, Joe was deeply touched. "That was so nice of you, Marley," he kept saying.

But he was seeing a person who did not exist, because she was not really very nice.

She looked at Joe and planned their lives, while he thought of nothing except a brown ball bouncing on a yellow floor.

Dad had married a woman who had slowly turned into somebody else entirely. All Dad had left of his original marriage were the wedding photographs and the early furniture.

Marley was reversing the scheme. She was somebody else right from the beginning. It was fun, like stepping into costume for every date.

At halftime Joe turned dizzily and said, "Wow. Those guys can play. Gonna be a great season."

Marley was wearing charcoal wool shorts with white tights that beautifully showed off her long legs. Joe failed to compliment her. Instead he recapped the first half, making sure Marley understood the fine coaching.

Marley said, "I've been thinking about New Year's Eve. Where should we celebrate?"

For a man who had had eight years of college, he looked remarkably dumb. She could actually see his little gears shifting, his teeny brain attempting to get out of basketball and into life. For a minute she did not even like him, and during that same minute he did not like her.

It was a minute in which they could have broken up. It would not have damaged either heart. It would just happen, and they would move on and forget each other.

But with an effort Joe said, "New Year's Eve. Yup. Be here soon."

"I love New Year's Eve," said Marley. "It has to

be a really special event we'll remember all our lives, because it will be our very first New Year's Eve together."

Joe scanned the basketball court, in case half-time was over and the teams were bounding out. No such luck. "The event to remember all our lives will certainly be your mother's. We'll hit the solstice. I'll wear my tux. You'll wear the black dress that makes you look like a goddess. And we'll find out what those stones are, and I'll even dance. I promise."

Marley was appalled. Show up in her own hometown, among people who had known her all her life, and watch while they laughed at Edith? "Never," she said.

"I want to meet your family," he pointed out. "I might as well see your mother in her normal setting, which apparently is a rock quarry. And Sophie, who has *been* a rock, I definitely want to meet Sophie."

Marley had no use for Sophie right now. Marley had assigned Sophie the job of staying sane and calm. By example, Sophie was to prompt Mother and Dad into better behavior. Sophie was known in the family for her quiet, slow manner. Marley had always thought Sophie would be a fine dog trainer.

And had Sophie agreed to commit Mother to an asylum once she had started naming rocks in fields? Did Sophie say she had found a good psychiatrist? Or even a *lousy* psychiatrist? Or one single little tranquillizing pill?

No.

Sophie was busy falling in love with a loser.

Of course Marley had not seen Ted since Ted was thirteen, and she tried to make allowances for the terrible age of thirteen; tried to believe Ted had improved, because all boys improved between thirteen and sixteen. After all, they couldn't get worse. But she doubted if this had happened in Ted's case. "No," said Marley. "We are not going to that solstice thing."

Joe gave her a kiss. "Your family sounds so interesting, Marley. Come on, it's one weekend. You can stand them that long. We'll pretend it's a circus."

"It *will* be a circus," said Marley, who wanted to break down and weep. People will accept Dad no matter how disgusting it all is, she thought, because his little second wife is adorable and he'll get points for her. But people will laugh at Mother. I can't stand the idea of being laughed at. It makes me remember seventh grade.

"We'll help your mother," said Joe, "bail out your sister, calm your father."

"Murder Persia," added Marley.

Joe laughed as if this were a joke. And then he forgot Marley, because the second half began and the score was close.

But long before solstice, Marley had to face the Thursday formerly known as Thanksgiving, with the People Formerly Known as a Family. Marley resolved to be nice. She had done it once, she could do it again.

On Thanksgiving morning Ted woke up too early. He couldn't even have breakfast, because relatives were asleep on pullout couches all over the place and nobody would be thankful if he woke them up.

He yanked on jeans and several shirts, since he no longer had a jacket, and went out into the dark. There was no moon and not yet sun. It was just hard morning cold that would chap his lips and hands.

He spoke softly to the dogs in their wire enclosures and they whined eagerly, wanting to join him, but he walked alone down the lane that circled the quarry, and turned uphill.

Frost had silvered the meadow. Old dry grass brushed against his jeans, whispering of what had happened in the night. The bare fingers of trees bent down, and the wind cried out, and Ted, shocked, realized that Edith was right. There was a complete circle. *I can see all of the stones, even the ones that aren't there.*

But they were deer, which slipped away and were gone. There were no mysteries up here, never had been.

Ted glanced up at a crunching sound, expecting deer.

Granddad stood on the henge. He was backlit by sunrise, motionless and grand. His cap was tilted, his big old hands knotted.

Granddad, Ted thought. Then he said, "Hi, Dad."

"Weather forecast is hard freeze tonight and Friday," said his father. "We can move Old Number Five Saturday. Won't tear up the ground so much."

"That's great!" said Ted excitedly. "Did you call Mrs. Olivette?"

"At dawn on Thanksgiving morning?" said his father. "Anyway, she's your call."

This was a terrible thought. Who would want Edith Olivette for a responsibility? "Dad," Ted said hesitantly, "I never know what I'm thinking when I'm with—well, with the Olivettes." He knew exactly what he was thinking when he was with Edith. It was Sophie who blurred his vision.

"I know what I'm thinking." His father's squinty eyes, wrinkled by years of sun and sand, got squintier. "I'm thinking you lead a much more interesting life than your brothers ever did. Your granddad would love this. If a guy could visit from the grave, he'd be visiting."

Ted squinted into the rising sun the way Dad did, yanking the corners of his eyes together.

"You're not supposed to have favorites," said his father, "but you were your grandfather's favorite. He was real sorry when he knew he would die and you were only eleven. He said he'd never know what you did with your life."

Tears flecked Ted's eyes the way mica flecked the surface of granite.

When they reached the house, Ted could hear

the giggles of his little nieces and nephews and the pounding of their feet, chasing around the kitchen table. In the Larkman home, there would be twenty-three people to be thankful for today.

"Dad," said Ted, just before he opened the kitchen door, "I don't want Mrs. Olivette and Sophie to be nuts and broke."

"It's their destiny," said his father. "They're already nuts. They'll be broke in a couple of weeks."

Ted couldn't laugh. How was Sophie doing, on her first Thanksgiving with nothing to be thankful for?

Real life had a way of making promises invalid. In ten minutes Marley lost the slightest desire to be nice. As if looking like a hag was not enough, Mother actually demonstrated how she danced around field stones. She did this in public. In a restaurant. On Thanksgiving.

"You seriously believe I would bring Joe home to meet the family?" Marley said to her sister. "What family? Neither of them qualifies as a parent."

The sisters were sitting opposite each other in a slick striped booth in a Chinese restaurant. It was the kind with good food but no atmosphere. Paper napkins and plastic flowers.

Marley and Sophie and Mother had spent a hideous afternoon cruising half the state to find a place for Thanksgiving dinner because Mother hadn't remembered to make a reservation. Sophie had had the nerve to say *Marley* should have arranged dinner.

It had never crossed Marley's mind to consider the practicalities of Thanksgiving dinner away. Dinner was something other people achieved. Your mother, your friends' mothers, your restaurant staff. Marley had an unpleasant insight into marriage: somebody had to make dinner.

"Why doesn't Mother wear lipstick anymore? Or get her hair done?" demanded Marley.

"Because the Ancients didn't wear lipstick or get their hair done."

"That's completely not true," said Marley.

"Marl, don't talk so loud," said her sister. "And don't talk at all now, because here comes Mother back from the ladies' room."

Their mother was garbed in a ridiculous combination of skirt, shirt, overblouse, and scarves. Marley had had it. "Mother, you look awful. There's no excuse for it. You could exert yourself a little. If you studied art history, you would know that in ancient societies, looks mattered. Women used eye shadow in Egypt, braided their hair in Assyria, painted their bodies in Ethiopia, embroidered their gowns in Pompeii. Everybody in every society at all times cared about their looks except you."

Her mother's cheeks grew very pink.

"There, see?" said Marley. "If you'd just wear a little blush, a little powder, it would take years off your face."

"I'm proud of those years," said her mother, "and I don't mind if they show."

"What's there to be proud of?" snapped Marley. "What do you have to show for them? Honestly, Mother! I agree with Dad. You're just a pyramidiot."

———∼∿∿∿∼———

Sophie was not actually angry at Marley for spitting out those words. They were true. And Mother did not have an excuse.

But neither did Marley have an excuse.

"Pyramidiot?" repeated Mother. Her face caved in, like something left out in the rain. "Is that what Daniel calls me?"

She still loves him, thought Sophie. She still cares what he thinks of her.

I have to rescue this. My tiny little remnant of a family, I can't let it die here. "You should see Mother in the stone circle, Marl. She even got Ted to dance."

Marley sighed heavily.

Sophie soldiered on, trying to get to the end of this terrible Thursday. "Marl, bring Joe to the solstice party."

"I want to marry the man, not scare him to death," said Marley. "If he sees what kind of family I come from, he won't want to have children with me."

Ah, the helpful voice of her sister; the only other person in the same boat.

And then Sophie thought: Marley's not in the

same boat. She's away and she can stay away. I am alone in this boat Mother and Dad and Persia have put me in.

"Marley, darling," said Edith, "my Solstice is going to be a wonderful party. Mrs. Larkman is renting tuxedos for Ted and Mr. Larkman, and they'll escort each person up the path, like wedding guests. Isn't that charming? And we'll have a hundred luminarias, fat candles safe in the sand at the bottom of little brown paper bags. I'm busy planning the decorations to cut along the top of each bag."

"This is Thanksgiving conversation?" said Marley. "Any decent mother would have shoved a turkey in the oven and given us something to be thankful for. You should be at a lawyer's office putting a stop to this. Or at an employment agency getting a job."

Mother's cheeks turned patchy red instead of pale pink. "Marley, darling," she said, "at first I was crushed when I realized the circle was not ancient. Then I understood that each stone was destined. They have been waiting centuries for the moment when they could join the circle."

Marley put her head in her hands. "Sophie, don't you see your responsibility here?"

"No," said Sophie, who saw it only too well. "You're the oldest, you take responsibility."

Soap operas are not about responsibility.

They are about irresponsibility.

I'll be a spinoff, thought Sophie. I'll leave my parents' soap opera and star in my own show. My show will have only nice people and happy endings.

Of course, it wouldn't have very good ratings. And it wouldn't stay on very long.

In soap operas, nice is boring.

Chapter 13

The Friday after Thanksgiving was supposed to be a sleep-late, slouch-around day. It was a day on which nothing should happen. Sophie would poke in the refrigerator and find nothing to eat, even though it was crammed with leftovers, and she and Marley would agree that they should have rented a movie.

But Persia and Dad were back from Thanksgiving with Persia's family and wanted to talk about it, which meant Sophie was hiding in her room.

If this lasted much longer, she was going to have to buy a rope ladder and come and go through the window.

Then she remembered that No, it was not going to last much longer.

Sophie forced her mother to get dressed. Mother scurried downstairs, where Persia and Daniel were waiting, hoping to exchange Thanksgiving memories, but she fled to the car, so Sophie had to go alone to find Dad and ask for the key.

"Hey, great!" said her father, beaming. "You're going to look at the apartment at last. I was starting to worry."

"I'm glad to hear it," said Sophie. "You should have been worrying all along."

"Aw, Soph, give me a break. Listen, what did you do for Thanksgiving? The fridge is empty. You go to a restaurant?"

"We had Chinese. I need the key." In her right hand Sophie held her key chain. Its leather handle, made by an eight-year-old Marley in summer day camp, had Sophie's initials burned into it. Sophie had been too little then to own any keys. The leather oblong had waited on her dresser for years.

"Here," said Dad, "I'll put it on your key ring for you." He reached out to take Sophie's keys from her and she was overwhelmed; horrified. He would remove the key to this house. He would say, You don't need this anymore. You don't need your family or your front door.

Sophie snatched the key out of his fingers. She heard Persia calling her name but she did not look up and she did not answer.

In the Land Rover, Mother had the engine going, the interior heated and the radio on. But she was in the passenger seat, staring ahead like a person in a dentist's chair.

Sophie rarely drove. Mother wouldn't let anybody else touch the Land Rover, and when Sophie drove the Volvo, she felt like an old lady with children of her own and shirts to take to the dry cleaner. As for the Z3, Sophie had never touched it. It might as well have had a blinking neon sign—DIVORCE EXIT VEHICLE.

There was nothing to say to Mother. This drive, this new key, this new building in which they would hang their coats: these were Edith's choices. And Edith was going to let somebody else take her there, just as she had let Daniel dictate the last few months.

At the apartment complex, there was no place to park except narrow slots for small vehicles. People here did not own bulky Land Rovers. These, definitely, were apartments with a reasonable rent.

Sophie opened the door to number eleven.

Inside, chilly and damp, the way unoccupied places were, was a wide white room with dark green carpet. No fireplace, no built-in bookcases. Just two large rooms. A kitchen window that looked at parked cars. Upstairs, two plain bedrooms, four small closets, and one and a half tight bathrooms.

It wasn't meant to be perfect. It was meant to be a roof and a stove and a place for a bed. Where people kept a toothbrush, not a family.

"It's not that bad," said Sophie. Her voice echoed in the emptiness. "It's white and green. It's clean and fresh. Marley will come. We'll be okay."

Lies, all lies.

She felt a scraping fear of January. Would Dad

really support them? Once he was in France, or Egypt, or wherever, would he think of them?

One of the bedrooms was big enough for sharing. Sophie would take it and hope for the best. Marley did have four weeks' vacation over Christmas. Would she come? Would she stay?

"We'll keep the Christmas ornaments," she said fiercely. "Especially the ones Marley and I made in Sunday school. We'll deck the halls with boughs of holly, Mother. We'll take the sound system and the CDs. We'll have music."

Her mother had trouble with the stairs. Halfway down, clinging to the rail, she said, "Sophie, I don't hear music anymore."

When they got back to the house, Persia had moved the car up to the front door and was stowing things inside it. Sophie could see Dad in the front hall.

Mother went inside by the garage, shoulders dragged down and eyes averted. *I don't hear music anymore.*

Dad was knee deep in new luggage, admiring the soft buttery leather and sliding the paper out of the beautifully designed luggage tags so he could fill in name and address. "Hey, sweetheart," he said cheerfully.

Sophie believed that a condemned man should have a last chance. She got right to the point.

"Daddy, this is so awful, this splitting up. Please don't divorce. Don't remarry. I need you."

"Soph, I'm the needy one. Can't you see how wonderful Persia is for me?"

What she saw was his selfishness. But was Mother any different? She had put her passions ahead of her family for years. And Marley always put herself first.

I'm the whole family, thought Sophie. Everybody else is single. "Daddy, what about us? Don't we matter?"

"You matter tremendously. You're my baby girl and I love you. I'll buy you presents wherever Persia and I travel. You'll get postcards from all the cathedrals and castles."

"Dad, this isn't about getting mail."

"Sophie, if you're worried about your mother, she's a teacher, she can get a job in ten minutes. This will be good for her. She'll have to throw off her nonsense and be an adult again." He shifted the suitcases, eager to move on.

"Where are you going?" asked Sophie.

"Persia and I are off for the rest of the weekend. Break in the luggage. You know."

"Dad," she said desperately.

"Aw, Soph. I know you love your mother, but Edith's computer hasn't been connected for years. I know marriage is supposed to be for better or for worse, but I couldn't keep up."

"It isn't the marriage!" she cried. "It's the family. Who's left to ask how my day went? Or what I want for dinner? Or whether I'm worried about college entrance exams?"

Persia beeped the horn.

Dad hoisted garment bag and suitcase, carry-on and camera. "Persia and I have a plane to catch, honey. You can handle this beautifully, I know you can. I'm counting on you."

Sophie shut the door so she would not have to watch them drive away. It was utterly silent, as if the house had died.

So, Dad, she said to him, you lost your chance. Because guess what? I do know somebody with a bulldozer. I can bring Ted around. I don't care if my plan has loose screws. I am going to bulldoze your plans, Daniel Olivette. You're not going to be able to hear music anymore either.

●—◁WW▷—●

Ted was alone at the circle. He could hardly wait for tomorrow, when the crew would come in (and earn Saturday overtime) and they'd move Old Number Five. And then, maddeningly, Mrs. Olivette drove up in her Land Rover. She leaped out, holding a rust-colored hat with a large flopping brim to her head with one hand, and in the other hand . . . her lute.

Things can always get worse, Ted thought.

"Look, Ted!" cried Edith. "An eagle! Paying homage!"

It's a hawk, thought Ted, and it sees a mouse.

Out of the woods and over the grass came Sophie. She wore scarlet leggings—and his jacket. The wind caught her hair. He thought of her hair as brown, but now he saw it was a dark, hidden red.

If his parents separated, Ted would crack like slate hit by a sledge. Sophie had not cracked. Well, unless you counted wanting to bulldoze your house. That was somewhat cracked.

Maybe Ted could talk Sophie into a backhoe. Dad would let him park a backhoe on the Olivettes' grass. A backhoe was plenty capable of destruction, but it had rubber tires and could be driven on a road.

But the word *backhoe* didn't have the power of the word *bulldozer*. A backhoe was just machinery at the wrong address. Daniel and Persia wouldn't even guess it was Sophie sending a message of wrath.

"Hi, Soph," he called eagerly. "How was Thanksgiving?" he asked, and could have broken a lute. How did he think Thanksgiving was? It couldn't have been anything but awful. "Somebody goofed up the cooking assignments for ours," he said quickly. "There were seven pies and no vegetables. My little cousins were thrilled. No creamed onions."

"I'm so jealous. You have such a big family. You can gather and gather. Our family just dwindles away. They probably won't even be able to count us during the next census. We'll be an estimate."

You can be part of our family, he thought.

Ted leaned forward, struggling for the words to use with Sophie.

Edith began playing her lute.

Sophie had hoped to find Ted alone so she could advance her shiny new bulldozer plans.

But how clear it was to Sophie that Ted had come here to *be* alone. To plan his Saturday event. He could not do a test run. He had to shift Old Number Five right the first time, and fifteen-ton rocks were not known for their cooperation. The kind of guy who worked in a gravel pit would not be sweetly understanding if Ted screwed up.

The last thing Ted wanted right now was Edith's swooping around with her lute and Sophie making insane requests. Sophie tightened his jacket around herself, sorry she had worn it. He would misunderstand.

"I came to bring you home, Mother," said Sophie. "It's time for dinner."

Ted wanted desperately to invite them to dinner at his house. Friday after Thanksgiving—there was a ton of food. But Dad said at breakfast how wonderful it was to have a rest from Edith Olivette.

"How did this happen to us, anyway?" said his father. "Do you think she'll stop coming once her stone is in position?"

"You know what we could do?" said his mother. "We could wire the stones and then they really could talk to Edith."

"Don't pick on her," said Ted.

"Then don't bring her around," said his father.

So no matter how big the turkey carcass and how deep the bowl of leftover mashed potatoes, Ted could not invite the Olivettes for dinner. His parents were at the end of their patience. He didn't want Sophie to know just how much patience her mother required. He said awkwardly, "See you guys tomorrow, then. You're coming, aren't you, Sophie? To see me move Old Number Five?"

"I bought three disposable cameras, Teddy," Sophie told him. "I can take ninety pictures of you. And I will."

He felt like gold.

Sophie watched his long legs as he strode away, framed against purple shafts of sky and cloud. At the top of the lane, he waved. Behind him twinkled the tiny tree on the highest chute, the one for luck and for blessing. She waved back, her heart sliding down a chute of its own.

When he was out of sight, her mother grabbed her arm and gave it an angry jerk. "You're sixteen, Sophie!" Edith's face was twisted in anger.

Sophie stared, frightened in the twilight.

"Why couldn't you fix yourself something to

eat?" snapped Edith. "You have to come here and ruin my time alone?"

It was all Sophie could do not to wrench the lute out of her mother's hand and smash it over her head.

Here Sophie was, at every turn, trying to do the right thing, and now this other Person Formerly Known as Parent wanted nothing but time to herself. They both dared claim that Sophie should be fine without a mother or a father.

Pizza and solitude—that was enough! What was Sophie whining about?

Okay, so I won't bulldoze the tower! Let Dad have another life. Let Mother suffer. Who cares if she hears music?

Lies, all lies.

Sophie cared so much.

———-\/\/\/\-———-

Soap operas do not have long sweeping views of horizon and cloud, of incoming thunderstorms or sunsets curling over mountain ridges.

That's the Weather Channel.

The Weather Channel is so safe.

Weather solves itself, blowing away and turning into another day.

But family! They are blizzard and storm, drought and flood. And they don't blow away.

Chapter 14

Sophie's mother wore a black coat and gloves and a formal black hat with a stiff brim and ribbons. She rammed her yellow hard hat right down over the black one. She looked like a funeral director worried about concussion.

Mr. Larkman's gravel-pit crew were a rough crowd. But they loved Edith's hat and her dancing and excited yoohoos. They loved her applause and the way she shouted "Yay!" every time they did anything.

"They've never had an audience," Pam Larkman said to Sophie. "Hardly anybody comes to a gravel pit and cheers and waves a flag."

Sophie was working quickly through her camera supply. "Get me, get me!" the crew yelled, making muscleman poses around the rock.

Under the influence of Edith Olivette, the crew could act the way moving Old Number Five deserved.

Nuts.

The essential insanity of the whole thing was like a carnival on a good day.

How terrific Ted looked, frowning under his hard hat. Sophie loved how serious he was. She often spelled her thoughts as if they came off a keyboard. T, E, D space, she typed to herself. L, O, V, E, S space M, E period.

He had not, by any syllable or gesture, implied any such thing.

Ted's father was keeping a low profile. It wasn't easy for him. He was reduced to standing with Sophie, making small talk. "You know the scientific name of a boulder like Old Number Five?" asked John Larkman.

"No, what?"

"Glacial erratic," said Mr. Larkman.

"Good name," said Sophie. "If ever a bunch of erratics gathered together, it's us."

Stone dust sifted into their lungs and hair. The day was very cold. Sophie's fingers ached, but if she put mittens on she couldn't take photographs.

Ted climbed into the cab of a loader whose tires were as tall as Sophie. He was almost as cute from behind as from the front. She took several shots.

The window on the cab door had been hit by a rock and splintered outward in a thousand tiny pieces that had not fallen away. Ted was barely visible behind a star of broken glass. And unexpectedly, the awful edge of jealousy she had been feeling toward people with solid families went away. People were allowed to be happy. Even Sophie was allowed to be happy.

She felt like a little kid on a Ferris wheel when the sky was blue.

Two days late, Sophie lifted her face to the sky and gave thanks.

—◦–◦–◦–◦– ·–ΛΛΛ– ·–◦–◦–◦–◦–

Ted raised the bucket. The chains held and Old Number Five did not shift. Her winking diamonds of mica filled his entire window. Ted could not see around her. The crew walked ahead and on his left, yelling instructions.

On his right were the cliff and the skimpy wire of the old fence. Lying in the yard, Old Number Five had been tame. Vertical, she was a living thing. She wanted to throw Ted into the quarry pond a hundred feet below, like a stallion who hated a rider.

Through the splintered window, Ted saw Mrs. Olivette yank off her hard hat, and then her black-rimmed and -ribboned hat, and dance and wave her two hats.

The one thing she had to celebrate was the placement of a rock. In a few minutes, that stone would be in its circle, and then what? Would Edith find peace or lose her mind completely?

Ted Larkman offered a prayer for Edith Olivette, and then, as long as he was tuned in, a prayer that the feet of Old Number Five would slide neatly into their grave, instead of tipping and falling and smashing bystanders.

Sophie and Mrs. Larkman and Edith followed like a tiny parade. Mr. Larkman made them stand on top of the henge where they couldn't get in the way. The first day of winter might not have arrived, but this was winter wind, hunting out weakness.

Slowly, delicately, Ted lowered the great stone. The crew took off the chains, and Ted pushed her upright with the bucket, like an elephant using its trunk to shift its baby. Then the crew filled in around Old Number Five with rocks and soil and tamped it down with the baby backhoe. What had taken the Ancients weeks or months had taken Ted an hour.

Sophie got Ted's picture as he stepped down from the cab, laughing and swinging his hard hat. Perfect portrait. Ted, weather, machine, rock.

The November day was shutting down fast. Everybody had places to go and sensible things to do. The loader was driven back down. Mr. Larkman jounced off in the backhoe. The crew climbed into the open bed of a truck and vanished.

Edith and Pam Larkman and Ted and Sophie stayed.

There was no beautiful sunset. It just got dark, from the bottom up, like a rising tide. Four humans were in a row on top of the henge.

Five stones stood silent, four in a curve and one at a distance, giving depth to the circle that was not there.

Old Number Five was no longer a stone for

company picnics. She stood grim and high and bleak. Alone, like a leader or a priest.

It *is* a sacred site, thought Ted. It is my grandfather's grave.

Ted's grandfather had been about as peaceful as a pit bull, and would despise Eternity if he had to rest in peace. So Ted prayed: Keep your eyes on him, God.

When he pulled together, Sophie was looking at him gently, as if she knew.

"Let's go somewhere," he said to her. "Out. I don't know where. Where do you think? You want to?" I'm in high school, he thought, and I have the speech patterns of a three-year-old.

But Sophie flung her arms around him and said, "Yes."

●━━∿∿∿━━●

Sunday of Thanksgiving break, he and Dad went to an auction of used construction equipment. They didn't bid on anything. Dad just wanted Ted to recognize a good buy. Then, because they were on a roll, Monday after school, they went to a horse auction.

"Always wanted horses," said his father, "but your mother's not interested."

"Put up a barn where it wouldn't bother her and have 'em anyway."

His father shrugged. "What's the point? I like doing stuff she likes doing."

Sophie jumped back into Ted's mind. He didn't

know yet what she liked doing, because they'd been stuck with what Edith liked doing. He tried to think past Mrs. Olivette and the divorce toward a time when he and Sophie—

Wow, he thought. Me and Sophie.

Putting the names together made him dizzy and unsure.

On Thursday his father said, "We haven't had an Olivette to dinner in three or four days. You feeding them at the circle or what?"

Ted laughed. "I haven't found any hungry Olivettes up there this week."

"You stick with this Olivette crowd, son," said John Larkman, "you're gonna have your hands full."

He *had* had his hands full, and it had been pretty great.

Dad went into the TV room to watch the news, because he liked access to a nap on the couch. Mom stayed in the kitchen to watch, because she liked access to food. Ted alternated between parents and televisions, carrying homework and food back and forth. He was in the kitchen with his mother when Sophie walked in the back door as if she lived there.

"They're divorced," she said. "It happened without us. Dad went to the Caribbean, some island where you just walk in and sign and it's done. That was the plane he and Persia were catching last Friday. He didn't even tell us."

She was as thin as a pencil, standing there. Her clothes looked like somebody else's. Even her eyes looked like somebody else's.

Ted's mother clicked off the TV and patted the

chair next to her. Sophie walked over numbly and seemed to study the chair to figure out how to use it. "My mother and father are not married any-more," she whispered. Her tears spilled so fast and heavily that Ted was frightened.

Ted changed his mind about the bulldozer. Smashing things was good. Bringing houses down on people who hurt Sophie was good.

"Have a chip," his mother said kindly.

Sophie's life had just crashed and potato chips were all his mother could offer? "If you and Dad divorced," Ted said to his mother, "I wouldn't want potato chips."

"What would you want?"

"I'd want to bulldoze the house," said Ted.

"Hey," said Sophie. "That was my brilliant idea. You can't do it too. Anyway, I waited too long, Teddy. It's ruined. I can't stop them now."

"What brilliant idea?" asked Ted's mother.

"I wanted Ted to lend me your bulldozer," said Sophie, "so I could bulldoze the tower and show my father and Persia a thing or two, and even ruin their lives."

Ted's mother began laughing. It was the kind of laugh that could go on for days. "It *is* a brilliant idea, Sophie. If my husband left me for a twenty-one-year old, I'd do it in a heartbeat." She took an ice cream cake out of the freezer and hacked into it with a cleaver because she was too impatient to let it thaw. "Let's send out shower invitations, Sophie. A tower shower. Everybody gets to throw glass and brick."

"I love your family," Sophie told Ted.

Ted's mother passed around smashed wedges of ice cream cake. It was vanilla, with layers of crumbled chocolate cookie in between.

"Daniel and Persia have to be there. Horrified, furious and above all, helpless. Should we tie them up?" asked Ted's mother. "I know! That big oak tree. We'll strap them to the tree as the bricks come tumbling down. Ted, you'll drive up to get Marley. Bring her boyfriend. He'll want to know what kind of family he's marrying into."

Sophie dug out a spoonful of crushed cookie from the center of her ice cream. "Ted will also be marrying into my family, Mrs. Larkman. Of course, he wants to wait thirty years, but eventually, I will be your daughter-in-law."

"Thirty years?"

"While she's in prison," explained Ted, "for mowing down the neighborhood with a stolen 'dozer."

"I keep telling you," said Sophie, "it won't be stolen. I'll have your permission." Sophie raised the spoon to her mouth and its cold touch was more than she could manage. Trembling, she set the spoon back down. "Mrs. Larkman, how come my mother won't fight?" she asked, through yet more tears; through an open faucet of tears. "How come she won't stand up for herself? How come she doesn't care what happens to me?"

It was a fair question and Ted had found no answer to it. He liked Mrs. Olivette, but he sure didn't like that part of her.

"Ted," said Mom, tucking Sophie in against her, "your father needs you."

This was ridiculous; Ted's father was not the type to need anybody, especially not at seven o'clock in the evening when he wanted to rest in front of the TV news. Ted was about to argue when he grasped that his mother meant "Get out." Sophie had not come to talk to Ted. She needed a parent and didn't have one of her own.

So he got out.

He and Dad sat silently staring at crime scenes that had occurred in distant cities and weather taking place in other parts of the country. "Dad? Mom's trying to talk Sophie out of borrowing our bulldozer to knock down her house to stop her father from remarrying."

His father considered this carefully. "How is that supposed to stop Daniel from remarrying?"

"He'd be ruined financially," explained Ted. "He has to get back out of the house all the money he put in it to go abroad with Persia for a year."

"I don't see why Edith doesn't automatically get half the house and half of everything else, too," said his father. "Isn't that the law?"

"I guess it would be the law if Edith got a lawyer to enforce the law. But she won't get involved."

"So Sophie's going to smash everything with a bulldozer?" said John Larkman. He looked down at his huge rough hands, the hands that had been Granddad's and would be Ted's. "In that case," he said to his son, "I guess I'd better teach her how to use one."

In soap operas people race in and out of affairs, trials, journeys, murders, and stolen babies and never reach a pleasant spot to stay for a decade or two.

They don't need true love. They just need love on a Tuesday afternoon so they can kill it on Wednesday.

I don't want a romance that gets filmed and wrecked and replaced, thought Sophie.

I want Ted.

Chapter 15

The first weekend in December meant shopping and putting up Christmas lights and going to the first Christmas concert. It meant the first ski trip and the first time you could wear the new scarf and mittens and beautiful boots.

Therefore, the first weekend in December, Marley was busy. She refused to come home and help pack.

If Sophie had had a bulldozer right then, she would have skipped plowing through her father's house. She'd have taken Marley down. But all her life, Sophie had laid siege to the fort that was Marley and failed to win anything but the occasional skirmish.

At least Ash and Jem knew how people were supposed to behave. They were supposed to bring empty boxes and fill them. Ash remembered tape and Jem had bubble wrap and labels.

"This is just like Marley," said Sophie, wrenching open closet doors and exposing cubic yards of her sister's stuff. She reached into Marley's ocean of possessions and plucked out a tiny orange sweater with a purple wolf on it. "How am I supposed to know what she needs for the rest of her life? Her seventh-grade cheerleading uniform? Do we pack it reverently in fresh white tissue paper? Or chuck it in the trash?"

"Pack every single thing Marley has ever owned," advised Ash. "You don't need another fight. Rent a storage unit, one of those metal garages you get by the month. Charge it to your father."

Jem snorted. "What use has Marley been? This is revenge time. Attach a chute to the window. Pour all her stuff out the window into a garbage truck and send it to the dump. For the rest of her life, whatever Marley mentions, you get to say, 'Huh? Guitar? Yearbooks? Keyboard? Gosh, Marl, I don't remember anything like that.' "

"Jem, you're brilliant," said Ash admiringly. "You came up with the bulldozer idea, too."

"I don't *look* sick and twisted," said Jem proudly, "but I come through."

"I have a bulldozer appointment tomorrow," said Sophie, "but regrettably I am not acquainted with major trash haulers."

Ash and Jem laughed. They literally did not believe that Mr. Larkman was taking Sophie bulldozing. They didn't even ask questions; this had to be a joke they hadn't caught on to. When Sophie said, "Ted Larkman's family is helping my mother handle things," it never occurred to Ash and Jem that Ted was anything other than a name to identify his parents.

This was probably just as well, because every time Sophie thought about Ted, she wanted to sob. There was enough to sob about. She didn't need additional sob situations lining up waiting their turns.

They hadn't done much on that lovely date after that silly stone shifting. Drove around a lot and talked about families. Eventually, Ted kissed her. They had neither of them done this before. It turned out to be a skill that required practice. So they practiced.

No wonder people wanted to do this, and then do it again.

But when he took her home, he just said, "See you," and drove away.

He did not call the next day. Did not search her out in school on Monday. The days passed. When Sophie fled to the Larkman house with her divorce announcement, Mrs. Larkman came through for her. But Ted went and watched television.

That whole "I'll be your other two feet" thing—Ted had just been trying to steady the quivering remnants of a family.

Last night, somewhere toward dawn, Sophie had realized that there was no difference between her pain and Edith's. They were both crying to a sky and a world: Somebody love me. Love me best.

Sophie liked sorting through her possessions, holding each one, and remembering—or not remembering—its place in her life. She liked the neatness of boxes lined up the way life ought to line up—all labeled and square—but never did.

"I could make a career of this," said Sophie. "You're busy, you have a tiny skill, you get tired, and the day is over. You survived."

Survival was key.

December was hurtling forward the way December did. The minute you scrubbed the turkey pan after Thanksgiving (if only Sophie had had that privilege) you tumbled headlong into December. They would be packed, moved, solsticed, and Christmased in no time. And then wham, a new year and a very new world.

"How was your Thanksgiving?" Ash asked Jem.

"Perfect. We do the exact same thing every year. I love Thanksgiving the way it always is, even the things I never eat."

The beauty of things the way they always were. Sophie had lost that forever.

—WW—

Sophie and Mr. Larkman drove to the job site in his red Dodge Ram. He was putting in a road. The trees had been logged and the stumps yanked up, but there were hills, ravines and shoulders or rock to scour away. Mr. Larkman lurched through mud and ditches, crushing small branches beneath his wheels.

"Ted isn't coming?"

"Nope."

There stood the fifty-ton 'dozer, silent in the

broken woods. It was monstrous. The blade was wider than her bedroom and as high as her shoulder. Mr. Larkman climbed up on the huge tracks, and Sophie climbed after him. The cab door was hanging open. No lock, not even a latch. There was one seat. "Siddown," said Mr. Larkman.

Sophie should never have come.

Machines were for Ted's kind of person. Dreams were for Sophie's kind. She did not want to touch these levers sticking out all over the place. Turn controls, blade controls, forward and reverse. Mr. Larkman gave her a tremendous amount of information, which she forgot instantly. She wanted to run, but the only way out was over the moving tracks, and having her feet caught in the bulldozer treads was not a great way to start the season.

The key didn't even start the engine but just warmed the battery. Separately, she had to turn the starter, and then the engine roared into existence. Brutal sound filled the cab and her head and her thinking. A spurt of blue haze exited the pipe sticking up on the front end of the cab, and its little cap jounced up and down.

Crushing Sophie's hand under his, Mr. Larkman made her practice shifting the blade. Then he bellowed, "See how the land goes uphill?"

Sophie saw.

"We're gonna call that hill Persia. You're going to skim Persia away, Soph. She's gonna be landfill."

Mr. Larkman folded against the ceiling of the cab, and with his fingers guiding her, Sophie adjusted the throttle and put the bulldozer into forward gear. The blade gathered everything: bush, vine, rock, dirt. It had no speed, just force. Inch by inch, they ate out the hill and walked the debris toward a ravine.

With his hands steering hers, they reversed and attacked the hill again. Over and over they peeled away hill and tipped it into hole. The noise and demand of the bulldozer made it hard to think. Divorce meant nothing. Even Ted receded. Only balancing the blades mattered.

Mr. Larkman took his hand away. Sophie made the next pass on her own. She was so proud she wanted to jump up and down like Edith at the circle, waving her hats and her flags. Where there had been a split in the earth, there was something solid; Sophie Olivette's landfill.

"Okay, turn it off," yelled Mr. Larkman.

One push on the handle and the bulldozer was motionless.

Sophie was dizzy from the quiet and clumsy getting down. She put her fingers on a metal shoe that would have severed her hand a minute ago. The change from monster to object was shocking.

Sophie surveyed her work. Half a hill remained. It looked like Mrs. Larkman's ice cream cake, sliced off with a cleaver. She and Mr. Larkman trudged toward the Dodge Ram. Sophie was so tired it took two tries to scrabble up into the truck.

"So, Soph," said Mr. Larkman, "you can't bulldoze your parents into behaving the way you want them to."

"I admit it. I want my life to come paved and

smooth. I don't want to have to yank out stumps or fill ravines."

"I don't know any lives like that," he said.

They drove in silence until they reached Sophie's house. The driveway with its square cobblestones curved among dark hollies, heavy with red berries. Its perfect roofline stretched over pillars and porches and welcoming doors.

"Toughest thing on earth is to stand by an embarrassing parent," said John Larkman. "I know, Sophie. I had one. You think it was easy in high school when my father put forty of my classmates into harness and made us drag large boulders up steep hills?"

It had certainly never crossed Sophie's mind that John Larkman had been a kid.

"You've got *two* embarrassing parents, Sophie. You don't seem to be letting either of them down. You impress me."

She got out of the truck.

Mr. Larkman squinted. "By the way. Ted wanted to come. I said next time."

She was coated with grit, so she came in through the fern room, whose slate floor she could not ruin. Kicking off sneakers that had aged a lot in one day, she went to the sink where the watering cans were kept. In the mirror, she saw a face so soiled it looked bruised.

But now she felt she had two possible futures:

moving-van packer and heavy-equipment operator. In each occupation, you were so tired at the
end of the day, if you had troubles at home, you
didn't even recognize them. You just fell over and
slid into a coma.

Dad and Persia emerged from the tower, hand
in hand.

Wrong, thought Sophie. I recognize my troubles just fine.

Her father wore a white turtleneck under a
dark jacket, like a man going to the symphony.
Persia wore a short pale sheath of ivory brocade.
Her splendid hair had been woven into circlets
and adorned with tiny white velvet bows.

They did not notice that she was filthy and
carrying the hard hat Mr. Larkman had given her
for a souvenir. They were far too busy gazing at
each other.

Truth came to Sophie like a blow from a
fourteen-foot blade. They loved each other. It was
wrong, it was sickening, it was true. How could
love be so unfair? Why couldn't people be swans,
faithful till death? How dare any love but the first
love exist?

"Sophie," said her father. "I want you to be the
first to know. Persia and I could not wait for New
Year's Eve." He laughed a high, excited laugh,
hugged Persia and said, "We just got married."

───∿∿∿───

It was a surprising turn for a soap opera, because it meant one less party.

The second wedding would have been good for a whole week of episodes.

How lucky—how lucky, lucky, lucky they were—on television.

Sixty minutes and it was over.

Sophie was stuck with her father's remarriage and her father's second wife and it was not going to be over.

It was a permanent episode.

Chapter 16

"Mother. Stop crying. The moving men are here. Pick up your list. Tell them what to take. If you wanted to stop this, you had plenty of time. You refused. Now stop whimpering. We're not going to cry in front of them. We're going to load furniture and boxes."

Her mother fled.

Sophie faced the moving men as calmly as she could and then burst into a torrent of sobbing, the kind that might take root and turn black and bottomless.

The moving men stood silently in the hall, waiting for her to be done.

"It's a divorce," explained Sophie, to excuse herself.

They shrugged. "We knew. You said you were taking only some of the furniture. Plus you're going to a crummy address. That's what divorce is. Somebody stays in the good place and somebody goes to the crummy one."

I impress Mr. Larkman, she thought, trying to steady herself.

"What do we take?" said one of the men. "Just point, you don't have to talk."

So Sophie pointed, and it went quickly, when you considered that it was the end of a life.

Mother came back, in a ghostly way, to hang along the edges of the move.

"Oh, Sophie!" she cried, when the lute and the pyramid books had been taken. "I was so conceited. I really thought I could just wait the affair out and my marriage would still be here. *My* Inner Self was better than *her* Inner Self, and Daniel would see and come back. But there was never a chance to save our marriage. What kind of marriage is it where my husband has to build a tower to get away from me?"

As each chair was turned upside down and stacked on top of another inside the van, Sophie felt herself turned upside down, leftover family emotion falling out of her pockets for strangers to walk on.

Persia walked in.

Sophie slammed shut the falling memory book of her life. "Get out of here, Persia," she said. "This isn't hard enough without the second wife watching?"

"Hello, Sophie," said Persia courteously. "Hello,

Edith. I won't be in the way. But I have to wait for the buyer. As soon as you're out, he's coming to measure each room for his own furniture." She was shivering with excitement. She literally stood on the threshold of her new life.

"Persia," said her mother, "I want to be sure I can expect you and Daniel at the Solstice party. You know it's the evening of the twenty-first."

I do not believe this, said Sophie to herself.

Persia actually hugged Mother. "Oh, yes! We want to come! Thank you, Edith, that's so thoughtful." Persia gave a little hop. "I love to dance. I can't wait to buy a dress."

Sophie stomped outside. It had rained earlier, and then frozen, and the cobblestones were slick and treacherous.

Ted had arrived in his truck to carry Marley's stuff to the storage unit. He was packing tennis rackets, bike, books, saddle, cheerleading pompons, ancient tricycle and Fisher-Price toy barns. He had old towels and torn blankets for padding and treated Marley's junk as if it mattered.

Sophie faded when she watched Ted. He had called, finally. "Hi," he'd said, "I want to help. Give me a moving assignment."

Was this the person who had snuggled with her in that very truck? The person to whom she had given her first kiss? And her second and her third?

I'm getting a dog, she thought. They're loyal.

Finally, desperate, she said, "I should come with you, in case there's something to sign."

Ted shook his head. "Soph, you don't want to see this place. This isn't even my stuff and I'm already depressed. It's hundreds of metal cubes with cement floors. It's like prison for things you used to care about."

He did want to be her other two feet. But it was stability he was offering, not affection. It's okay, Ted, she thought, you don't have to love me, I'm just glad you're here.

Daniel came bounding out of the house to greet the arrival of three cars. The buyer and family. The wife was a painter who would use the tower for a studio, and the husband was a pilot whose hobby was cooking. The sons were teenagers who loved the entertainment room. The house was perfect for them. The papers would be signed and the house would be theirs in ten days.

Sophie got into Mother's Land Rover and stared at the car phone. She could call Marley and beg. Marl, we need you. At least be here for the first night.

But Marley would yell, and it was too late for yelling.

It seemed like hours before Mother arrived at the car and they could actually leave. Sophie's insides felt crushed. If she went to the emergency room, they'd say: Trauma. Cracked bones, broken heart. "I can't believe you invited Dad and Persia to the solstice."

"I had to."

"Had to! Mother, where do you get this nonsense?"

"Sophie, I want to be at peace. No matter what it takes."

"It's taken everything," Sophie told her.

Ted packed Marley's stuff into its holding cell as if it mattered.

It was almost two weeks since the Saturday of shifting stones and kissing Sophie.

The phase of bumping into her at the circle was over. Nor would he see her by accident in school. They did not occupy the same wing at the same hour and did not have the same lunch.

Ted had promised himself he would talk to her today, during the move. But it was impossible. The place was filled with strangers and emotion. And he could not discuss his own emotions.

He could not begin to explain how queasy he felt around Daniel and Edith. The utter selfishness of them! If it was frightening to Ted, how must it be for Sophie? Ted was the only one who did not blame Marley for staying away.

Every day, he told himself he'd call Sophie. Every day, something happened to give him a chill. Like last week, one morning Ted's mother and father had had a serious argument, bad enough for each of them to leap in a car and drive away much too fast, as if they weren't coming back. He wouldn't have given it a thought if he hadn't been embroiled in the Olivette situation. Parents yelled and then they made up.

Except when they didn't.

Sometimes Ted couldn't be close to Sophie's divorce. After all, Sophie too had believed in her parents' marriage.

Sophie.

In school, talk between guys about girls was very dismissive. A girl meant a little bit, but not a whole lot, and there were so many to pick from. No need to get overly involved. Just move on. Ted understood why you had to be casual about girls. Anything else was risky.

But as he closed the door on Marley's stuff and fastened the lock and pocketed the key, he knew he had inherited something from Granddad and Dad other than huge hands and a gravel pit.

He could not be casual.

School in December was always exciting, with band concerts and one-act plays, choral concerts and early basketball games, final exams and art exhibits and applications for January SATs. Sophie trained herself to lead all her life at school and none at the apartment.

She could not bring herself to touch its walls. The bedroom that she was not, after all, sharing with Marley, was crammed with her stuff, but she felt like a camper. Nothing fit, nothing got comfortable.

Dad had not come over.

Sophie had gone back, collecting this and

that, and Persia had asked her to knock before she came in.

Late in the afternoon of December twentieth, the doorbell rang. Sophie was in her room doing homework. Mother had just gotten home from the circle and come running upstairs to tell her that the caterer's tent was set up in the field outside the henge and Porta Potties were hidden on the far side.

They were startled by the doorbell. They had not even known the apartment had one.

"I look awful," said her mother, as if it might be neighbors, with coffee and casseroles; as if this were the kind of place where neighbors even knew you were new.

But Sophie took advantage. It was a step in the right direction. "Put on that nice blue sweater, Mother."

"All right," said Edith nervously.

Sophie ran downstairs to peek through the spyhole before she opened the door. For years, she'd had an entire glass tower from which to spy. Now she had an eighth-inch pinhole.

It was Dad and Persia.

Sophie almost didn't let them in. She almost pretended nobody was home. But what was the point? She opened the door. Every time she thought it could not get worse, it got worse. She had to invite her own father into her own house. "Have a seat," she said.

"We won't stay long," he said.

Sophie could feel herself trying to be a good

daughter: helpful, kind, all the stuff Marley had abandoned. "We had auditions for the February musical, Dad," she said. "If you get a part, you find out this week so you can work on your lines during Christmas vacation." Ask me if I tried out. Ask if I got a part. Ask what musical we're doing.

Her father said, "Look at this brochure, Soph. We're going to stay in a castle that Queen Eleanor of Aquitaine once lived in. It's a hotel now."

Where is a bulldozer when you need one? thought Sophie.

Edith came downstairs timidly. She let her husband usher her into her own kitchen, where there was a table. A flat surface for signing papers that Dad suddenly produced.

"Do not sign, Mother," said Sophie. "Get an attorney."

"Sophie," said her father, "this is between me and your mother and does not involve you."

What was the matter with these people? How could divorce fail to involve the children?

Edith held the pen in her hand and set it down and picked it up and set it down. Dad and Persia could not take their eyes off the pen. "Daniel," said Edith in a questioning voice. "If Marley hadn't brought Persia home that weekend, you and I would be looking forward to our anniversary next May."

Persia managed to smile. Daniel didn't.

"Wouldn't we?" said Edith urgently, waiting for Daniel to say, Yes, of course, Edith, without Persia I would still love you.

"I would have divorced you anyway, Edith. I was only hanging on until the girls were grown," he said. "Persia just speeded it up a little. Now, will you just sign the papers?"

Get mad at him, Mother! Sophie thought. Then she took the pen out of her mother's fingers and said to her father, "I want you to leave. This is not your home and you were not invited." She did not raise her voice. She was stating a fact. "Get out or I'm calling the police."

"Sophie," said her father.

"You're a jerk," she said quietly. "And you're mean."

"Sophie, do not talk to me like that."

"A father gets to tell his daughter how to behave," said Sophie, "but Marley is right. You are only the Person Formerly Known as Father." She hit 911.

"Okay, okay," said her father. "I realize this is a very emotional time and I wasn't diplomatic. I'm sorry, Soph. I'm not mean, honey, and I didn't mean to sound mean." He didn't meet her eyes to see how this had gone over. He turned to Edith. "I'm sorry I upset you, Edith. We'll be at the party tomorrow night, and I'm sure we can smooth things over." He leaned forward, and Sophie thought, He's going to stick a kiss on Mother's cheek, like a stamp on a letter. Sophie got between them, the phone in her hand, and Dad and Persia left.

Her mother, as always, was no use. Forgot to be a parent. Trudged upstairs to be alone.

Sophie sat at the tiny kitchen table. I didn't try

out for the musical, Dad, she thought. I'm afraid to commit to four nights a week of rehearsals because I don't want Mother home alone that much. Why didn't you ask me, Daddy? Where did that father go, who used to take videos of everything his baby girl did onstage? Was he faking it all those years?

And tomorrow, at Mother's party, would he fake it again? Would he dare bring the paperwork that would sign everything over to him?

Yes. He would.

Sophie picked up the phone again and called Ted Larkman. "Teddy," she said, her voice ragged. "I need the bulldozer. I truly do. I hate him. I'm coming for the bulldozer. I'm taking him down. He and Persia are home. It's time."

"No," said Ted.

"Yes!"

"Sophie, maybe I could come over and we could go to a movie."

"I don't care about movies! You should have asked me for a date weeks ago, anyway, and you didn't, and who cares, it's still my house and I can still bulldoze it. And I'm going to."

"Sophie, what did he do this time? What do you want me to do?"

"I told you! Let me have the bulldozer."

"No," said Ted. "Sophie, listen, you—"

Sophie hung up on him.

Her father was allowed to run over her with fifty tons of metal track; he could ruin her family and her life; but she wasn't allowed to ruin his life back. She was supposed to be good. She was supposed to have a nice attitude and help out and make sure papers got signed and mothers stopped sobbing.

Oh, to have power!

Sophie went to her mother's room. "Get up off the bed, Mother. We're going out for dinner."

"I can't. I'm not going out in front of people, Sophie."

"Get up, Mother," she said fiercely. "We're not going to be defeated. We're going to dress up, and you're going to fix your hair, and I don't care if you don't have mascara anymore, you'll borrow mine, and we're not going to talk about the past. We're going to talk about next year. How we're going to get jobs and how we're going to hear music."

In a soap opera, there have to be secrets and lies. Hidden mysteries. Dark pasts.

When I'm grown up, thought Sophie, I really and truly will have a dark past. And I will keep it from my children. I don't think we'll curl up just before their bedtime and they'll say, "Mommy, tell us again how you almost called the police when your parents got divorced."

I know one thing, thought Sophie. My children are hearing only happy stories.

Because I'm giving them a happy life.

Chapter 17

December twenty-first.

The winter solstice.

Guests parked down near the gates of Larkman Gravel. Ted and Joe the doctor—smash hits in their gleaming black tuxedos—walked groups up the hill and into the meadow, as if it were an outdoor wedding. It was very cold. People were padded and plump from layers of long underwear and extra fleece.

The luminarias were strange and beautiful on the top of the henge, and the utter darkness above and beyond was eerie and even threatening.

The guests were left over from Edith Olivette's lost passions. The bingo players were hefty and sharp-eyed and over sixty. They wore polyester pants in hideous colors. The bird-watchers had brought binoculars, just in case.

Persia divided the Solstice party, as autumn is divided from winter.

Her velvet coat tapered to her slender waist and then flared like a black tulip. It had both hood and cape, over which her golden hair cascaded. In her presence, every bingo player, every poet and potter, became young and lithe and eager to dance. In her presence, Sophie and Ash and Jem and Ted were toddlers who should go home and play with blocks.

Hand tucked in Daniel's elbow, Persia went from group to group, introducing herself. "I'm Mrs. Olivette," she said, and even the people who had planned to despise her found that she was too beautiful to dislike, and smiled back, and greeted Daniel cordially.

Edith had to stand at her own party while her guests congratulated her husband on acquiring a better wife.

Sophie surrounded herself with Ash and Jem. Ted could not get her alone. "We promised," Ash told him, "not to leave Sophie's side during her first public appearance with a stepmother."

Sophie wouldn't look at Ted. In the strange swirling light of candles, it would have been difficult for anybody else to tell. But Ted certainly knew. "Sophie," he said desperately, even if Ash and Jem were listening. "I *had* to say no."

But Ash and Jem were not listening.

"Ted, you're the only boy," said Ash glumly, scanning the crowd.

"I see lots of male persons," said Ted.

"I'm not counting retired bingo players in tan jackets with missing buttons. I still had a thread of hope for a New Year's Eve invitation," said Ash. "Now it's gone. Sliced through. I'll be alone on New Year's Eve."

"We can waitress at your family's party," Jem reminded her.

"I refuse to enter the New Year as a waitress."

"Sophie," said Ted. "Just backing it off the flatbed would crack every one of those cobblestones. That would be my responsibility. And—"

"Ted, I understand, you can't get into trouble, and I'm nuts to think of it. It's nice of your family to let my mother give a party here and it was nice of you to help on moving day. I'm grateful."

The "No" and the "Good-bye" were standing stones between them.

The sky went from purple to black, and the stars rushed to get there in time. Up their unknown streets they came, glittering by the hundreds.

"Hello," crooned Persia to every guest. "How delighted I am to meet you! I," she said, "am Persia Olivette."

Edith began dancing. People were embarrassed. Nobody joined her.

It was Persia who coaxed a guest to dance with her, and drew in another, until dozens of dancers trailed Persia. They followed her around the top of the henge and in and out of the standing stones.

"I could throw Persia off the cliff," Ted said to

Sophie. "She'd make a nice splat. Afterward, I'd just grind her up with the rocks and there'd be no trace. Persia would become a basement wall somewhere."

Sophie almost smiled, and Ted thought he might be getting somewhere, but Ash and Jem began plucking at his jacket. "Sophie! Ted! Who are they? Those adorable boys, name them!"

"I have no idea," said Sophie.

"Yes, you do. They're your guests. They're our age! Quickly! Identify them!"

"Their family is buying Sophie's house," said Ted. "I met them on moving day when Sophie was hiding out in the Land Rover. You want me to introduce you?"

"I want you to take me up to the cutest one," said Ash, "and say, 'Listen, you're new in town, so I'm going to be a real buddy and introduce you to the girl you're taking out on New Year's Eve.'"

"Okay," said Ted, laughing. He thought Sophie would come, but as Ash and Jem propelled him toward the two boys, Sophie slipped away.

●—␣▧▧␣—●

The boys thought it was pretty cool to be invited out for New Year's Eve like that. They accepted, even without a party to go to.

"Our party," said Ted helpfully. "It'll be here too. You can come." And so it turned out that he had invited Jem and Ash and two strangers, but he had not invited Sophie.

He paced in the grass, stood at the top of the

mound, stood at the bottom. He stood on top of Granddad. Finally he lay down in the grass where his grandfather was buried and stared up.

Granddad had not come here for the sun, the moon and the stars. But Edith had. And she had been eclipsed.

Ted made a decision. He hoped it was not the stupidest decision of his life, but it was, and he knew it. Ted got up. He wasn't the type to dust himself off, or check for grass stains, or worry about his cummerbund. He broke into a run. Once you decided to do something, do it.

How scary the stones were inside their earthen walls. Their shadows stalked Marley.

Beyond the henge were the bare penciled outlines of trees. The thin twisted black was vicious and grasping. It was impossible that they had had green leaves, or ever would again. It seemed to Marley that the trees, their branches, their roots, were starved.

And what could a sacred circle like this have been for, if not sacrifice?

Firstborn sons.

Fruits of the harvest.

Or trophy wives.

Surely it was all the same to stones. They wanted a sacrifice. The circle, the dark, the gaping quarry . . . all called for sacrifice.

Marley could not take her eyes off Persia.

Persia was a princess on a castle wall, gleaming under the silver moon. She seemed timeless and ageless. She wasn't as beautiful as a Helen of Troy or a Cleopatra, and yet war had been waged over her, and a family killed.

"I would kill to look like that," said Ash.

"I," said Marley, "would simply kill."

"Joe," called Ash. "Marley needs you."

Joe came loping over. He was shaped like an athlete without being one. His long legs slammed the ground inefficiently and his elbows banged his sides. But Marley did not tell him this. She was hit by a wave of grief for all people who pretended to be something they weren't.

Joe isn't pretending, she thought. He's a prince. The trouble is, I'm not a princess.

"Marley is considering the death of Persia," Jem told Joe, "and how to accomplish it."

"Yes," said Joe, "we've discussed that at length. I keep explaining that Persia will disappear across the Atlantic Ocean, and that's as good as death."

"It is not," said Marley. "She'll be in Paris, for heaven's sake. That isn't death, it's life."

●━〜〜〜━●

Sophie saw Ted on his back in the middle of the circle.

He was all shadow.

She knew he was thinking stone thoughts. How he had moved Old Number Five. Dreaming of stones six and seven. He was thinking of backhoes and excavators. He had been tricked into wearing formal clothes, but he was lying there in overalls and steel-toed boots.

She looked where he was looking, into the universe. This is *Once upon a time,* she thought. This is where the stories begin: in the dark.

When she looked back into the grass, Ted was gone.

Ted ran down the hill and took the truck. There was too much action for anybody to notice him. Five miles to the job site. He spent the five miles telling himself not to do this. His father would kill him. He'd be sent to live with his older brothers for the rest of his high-school life. Unless he got the jail sentence he'd described to Sophie.

There was no traffic on back roads in winter after dark. He was there in ten minutes.

Don't get out, he said to himself. You're not the one who's supposed to be nuts and broke. Turn on the radio, go home.

He got out.

The fifty-ton bulldozer had been removed to the flatbed, ready to be delivered to the next site.

Leave it there, Ted said to himself. He jiggled the heavy key ring, not as heavy as his father's, but getting there, gathering key after key, responsibility after responsibility.

His father trusted him.

But Sophie had trusted him. He hadn't come

through for her. She had enough guts to face a divorce and a new life and never give up on her crazy mother. And the only thing he could say to her was, "No." She was right, he was gutless, hadn't even had the guts to ask her out.

He left the truck in the woods, got into the cab of the flatbed and drove to the Olivettes'.

Okay, at least leave the bulldozer on the trailer, Ted said to himself.

But how scary is a bulldozer on a flatbed?

I'll just move it onto the grass, he decided.

There was no such thing as "just moving" a bulldozer. Bulldozers had an impact.

Slowly he backed the big yellow bulldozer off the trailer. How he loved the power and the savage noise.

Soon, there were just a lot of little crunchy pieces where the cobblestones used to be. Another minute, and there wasn't much landscaping left. He chose the exact center of the three-acre lawn. Behind him in the grass were deep distinctive tracks, like a grizzly in the snow: a very large machine had passed this way.

The mansion was equipped with motion sensors, and as he approached, spotlights came on. He angled the tracks so they were centered on the tower, lifted the blade to its most threatening position and forced himself to shut the engine down.

The bulldozer gleamed, its shadow huge and black, and then timers turned the spotlights off and the bulldozer disappeared in darkness. But when Daniel and Persia drove in, their brights on, the shadow would be cast against the house, the perfect awesome silhouette of destruction.

The key chain was too large to slide into the tight pocket of his dress pants, so he dropped it into his jacket pocket, where it felt awkward and unsafe. Keeping one hand over the keys so they wouldn't fall out in the woods, Ted ran the route Mrs. Olivette used to approach the sacred circle on foot. He read his watch in the dark: the whole thing had taken forty-five minutes.

He burst out of the woods and into the meadow. He couldn't wait to tell Sophie, but he could wait a century or two before telling his father.

The party had moved into the caterer's tent. People wanted light and heat, not stone and cold. The musicians continued to play, though, and there were a handful of dancers. He did not find Sophie.

Ted danced with his mother, who did not notice that he was out of breath, excited and filthy.

He danced with a poet, he danced with Edith, he even danced with Marley. He could pay no attention to them, even when they demanded attention. He could hardly hear what Edith said, and he made a point of not hearing what Marley said. Where was Sophie?

Okay, he said to himself. A guy that deposits fifty-ton bulldozers in other people's landscaping can catch up to a one-hundred-ten-pound girl.

So he did.

"Let's henge, Sophie," he said, and he took both her hands before she could escape, and to his relief, she smiled. He was not sure of his feet, so he didn't bother to move them, but just fit himself up against her so closely they were two spoons stacked. "I did it for you after all," said Ted. "The bulldozer. You wanted a statement, you've got one. It's in your father's front yard."

"You drove the bulldozer over to the house?" she breathed. She linked her hands behind his neck and hung backward, staring up at him and laughing—happily, easily, lightly laughing. Then she danced around him and crossed his arms to pirouette beneath them. "Oh, Teddy! My father and my mother and my sister won't give me a thing. They just take." She kissed him on the lips. "You're the one who gave." He kissed her back.

"You shouldn't have done it," she said. "You'll be in trouble."

"Then what did you ask me to do it for?"

"Because I'm nuts and broke."

"I thought you had ten days to go. . . . Sophie," he said, with a thousand things to tell her before his father closed in and he really and truly was in fifty tons of trouble. But she was kissing him again.

Persia left the spiral of dancers, her candle flame illuminating her face and catching the dark romance of her velvet hood.

A rising wind put out the candle Persia held.

The wind rushed out of the trees and flattened the rest of the candles.

People shivered. They stopped speaking and stood still.

Marley smiled. The earth, the stones and some of the Olivettes deserved a sacrifice.

Marley's voice was soft and low, but the stones and the guests heard every word. "At night . . . when the solstice comes . . . and the year turns . . . the stones walk down to the river to drink."

They shuddered, even the people who knew there was no river.

"Go with the stones, Persia," whispered Marley. "They're calling you."

The wind made a queer slick sound against the distant quarry walls.

"It isn't far," said Marley. "Dance on, Persia. Dance off the edge."

But it was not Persia who began to scream. It was Sophie, wrenching herself from Ted as if she had been his prisoner, whirling in horror instead of joy. "Where's Edith?" cried Sophie. "She isn't here! She wouldn't leave the stones! Where's my mother? *Where is she?*"

People seemed to feel no urgency. Some continued to dance. Food was passed and drinks refilled. Sophie could have pushed them all into the quarry.

"Mother!" she screamed. How crushed was Edith? Sufficiently destroyed, on this evening of hopes gone wrong, to step off the side of one of those cliffs? While they were teasing Persia, enjoying a mean little moment in which she really was roadkill, had they left Edith unprotected?

"If something happened to my mother," said Sophie to Daniel Olivette, "if she hurt herself, or ran away, or if anything terrible or bad comes, it's *your* fault."

"Sophie, your mother invited us," said Daniel. "I'm sure she's around somewhere. She's behind a stone or something. Edith," he added, as if he wanted another piece of toast.

Sophie forced air into her lungs and shouted, "Mother!" but it was only a croak. She stomped her foot to clear her throat and yelled, "Mother!"

There was no answer.

Surely Sophie's soap opera was approaching the end of its season.

As each character left the stage for college, for the apartment, for France, the possibility of more episodes would dwindle.

Sophie, the invalid in the hospital bed, would be able to change the channel, look out the window, and even hop up and go to therapy.

But soaps go on and on, killing off this character and resurrecting that one.

In a soap opera, the episode of the missing mother would be shown on Friday afternoon, so you would have to wonder all weekend what had actually happened to the woman with the broken heart.

Chapter 18

"We have to organize a search," said Sophie.

"Soph, she's with Joe," said Marley. "Joe's a doctor, he knows how to calm people down, he can even calm me down."

What was so great about being calm? Sophie wanted to know.

"Now, Sophie," said Daniel. "Calm down. I'm sure Edith will feel better in a minute. I didn't know she'd be so upset when we asked her to sign the papers."

"You asked her now?" said Sophie. "Here, at her party?"

"I'm on a tight schedule," said Daniel. "I couldn't delay any longer. She had to get her act together."

"Oh!" said Ted Larkman, patting himself and generally looking foolish. "Oh, Sophie! I think she got her act together. I think she decided *she* couldn't delay any longer either."

Nobody was listening to Ted.

"Mother's okay, Soph," said Marley. "She was just upset when Dad tried to shove the pen in her hand. Joe was talking her into going for a cup of tea at the Larkmans'."

Ted grabbed Sophie's arms. "Sophie," he said urgently, "I danced with your mother. She's not calm and she didn't go to my house. When she was dancing with me, and I was telling her about changing my No to Yes, she said it was time for her to change her Yes to No. I think she picked my pocket."

"Oh, no!" said Marley. "She's stealing now? Ted, she wanted your change or something?"

"Of course not," said Ted. "She wanted my keys."

"Your keys?" repeated Sophie. Everything changed. Ted's keys—including the strange little duck profile key that started a Caterpillar. Sophie felt a crazy giggle surfacing. "Oh, Teddy! She's getting *that* act together? She won't know how to drive the bulldozer, though. I hardly figured out how, even with all that instruction."

"You *told* her how," said Ted. "You described every single minute of your whole lesson. She's not dumb, you know, just nuts. Dad!" yelled Ted.

"I'm here," said John Larkman.

"Dad, see, what happened is, I moved the bulldozer to the Olivettes' front yard. Just as a statement. And I happened to be discussing it with Edith. And—"

"You moved the bulldozer to the Olivettes' house? Which one?"

"The fifty-ton."

"She doesn't have a key," said John Larkman.

"She picked my pocket."

"First I'll stop her," said his father. "Then I'll kill you." John Larkman turned and trotted toward his house, Ted and Sophie at his heels.

"What's going on?" said Marley, following.

"Your mother's going to bulldoze the tower!" shouted Ted over his shoulder.

"Bulldoze the tower?" said Marley.

"That sounds familiar," said Jem.

"Bulldoze the tower?" said Daniel. "*My* tower? What are you talking about? Where would she get a bulldozer?"

Sophie's slippered feet pounded the sloping drive, her dress flying behind her, like Cinderella fleeing the ball before the magic ended. She was laughing the way Cinderella must have laughed, half thrilled and half terrified.

There was only so much drama a person could get out of pottery or pyramids. Mother was about to take up the passion that Mr. Larkman knew, that Ted knew, and that Sophie had felt for one afternoon.

Demolition.

Mr. Larkman unclipped from his belt a key ring so loaded he could surely start any vehicle in America. "Ted. Where's the Dodge?" he snapped.

"We better take a dump truck," said Ted, skipping the explanation of where the Dodge was.

"What's going on?" yelled Pam Larkman.

Ted opened the passenger door for Sophie and she vaulted in. "Edith's going to bulldoze her house, Mom," Ted said.

The matter-of-fact delivery of this sentence turned every guest into a believer. Edith Olivette was going to bulldoze her house. There was a flurry of people racing for cars, backing into each other, trying to get out, blocked by the badly parked cars of late-arriving bird-watchers.

John Larkman floored it.

Sophie was laughing. "Teddy, Mother got mad. There's hope." She took his hand and squeezed it.

Ted's father normally lugged along at twenty miles an hour, but tonight he drove as if in a race car. He was out of the truck almost before the ignition was off, and racing across the grass, but Edith had had enough time to figure out how to start the bulldozer, and she had found forward gear. An array of bright lights had come on to show her the way. She didn't need to change the blade. Ted had positioned it perfectly.

The lawn was wide and the bulldozer was slow, and nothing could stop that machine except Edith herself.

She looked quite wonderful up in the cab. Her hat was just right, a black tilt with a great soaring silver feather. The engine roared, and the puff of smoke flung the little cap in the air, and fifty tons of steel advanced upon the tower.

People catapulted out of cars and trucks, but they could do nothing. They could not vault up on the moving tracks of the bulldozer unless they wished to amputate their feet. They could not leap between the house and Edith unless they wished to be run over. There was no central power supply they could cut off.

"Edith Olivette!" bellowed John Larkman. "That black stick in front of you! Shove it forward! Stop that bulldozer right now!"

Cars slammed into curbs. Jem's car, Marley's car, Daniel's car, Mrs. Larkman's.

"Edith!" shouted Daniel. "Stop this!"

John Larkman began laughing. Sophie had never actually heard this sound. A chuckle, yes. But a laugh, no. John Larkman said, "Daniel. You lose."

"Go, Mom!" yelled Sophie, wishing she had Marley's old pompons. "That's the spirit!"

The blade scraped up landscaping. Before it tumbled maple and birch. Its progress was a symphony of ripping and tearing and wrenching. "You won't be in any trouble after all, Teddy," Sophie told him. "Mother will take the credit."

"Edith!" cried Daniel, running parallel to the bulldozer. "You can have your half! I'm sorry, okay? I apologize. Edith! Stop!" Daniel was pleading and wringing his hands, exactly as Sophie had dreamed. Persia was staring at the first wife she had thought was merely paperwork.

"Daniel, when Edith hits the tower, there will be a lot of glass," said John Larkman. "Stand back so you don't get killed."

The two adorable boys with Jem and Ash

gaped at the yellow apparition with its black-hatted operator. "Guess we're not moving here after all," said one of the boys.

"There'll be lots of souvenirs," said his brother. "You want bricks or glass?"

There were only a few yards between Edith Olivette and the tower.

Ted was so envious of Edith's being the driver and so grateful to be here and see the tower come down. The audience included the people who would laugh, the people who would be enraged and—a swirling light came around the corner—the people who would make the arrest.

"My house," moaned Daniel. "My house."

Pam Larkman said, "Actually, Daniel, it's half hers. It always was. That's the law in this state. And if she knocks her half down, the only legal difficulty is that she didn't get a demolition permit."

Marley said, "Ted. *You* helped her do this?"

Joe was yelling, "Place your bets, gentlemen!"

"I bet with bulldozing," said Sophie.

Marley said to her sister, "I take it back. Ted's not a dork carrying pebbles in buckets."

I like that, thought Ted indignantly.

"He's perfect, isn't he?" said Sophie, smiling at Ted. Ted had thought nothing could make him take his eyes off that bulldozer. He was wrong.

And then the world went utterly silent.

For when a diesel engine stopped, there was no afterward, no continuing vibration, no moment of idling. It just ended.

The tower stood untouched.

The bulldozer stood silent.

Daniel stood trembling.

Edith Olivette was not eclipsed.

There is true love, thought Sophie. I truly love my mother. I know exactly how annoying she is. I know exactly how childish and self-centered she is. And I wish she weren't. But I love her.

I never wanted to take sides. I don't think there should be sides when you're the kid. There should just be parents and love. But this is a divorce, and there is a side, and I'm taking my mother's.

Sophie left Ted. She crossed the shredded grass and stepped over the debris of broken trees. She held up her hand to assist Edith down. "You were awesome," she said to her mother.

"It was fun," said her mother. "I haven't had such fun in a long time."

"You haven't been a parent in a long time either," said Sophie.

They stared at each other, grown-up to grown-up, and then Edith Olivette put her arms around Sophie, mother to child. "You needed me," whispered Edith, "and I let you down."

Sophie nodded.

"Maybe you and Marley and I could do Thanksgiving over again," said her mother.

"And be thankful for what?" said Sophie gently.

"For daughters who love you anyway," whispered her mother.

The spell on the crowd broke, and they

surged forward, laughing and yelling and questioning and surrounding.

"You are crazy, Edith," screamed Persia. "You are certifiably insane! You need to be locked up."

"I have been crazy, Persia," agreed Edith Olivette. "I have been way too busy thinking exclusively of myself. I admit to a few months of derangement."

The police officer elbowed in, demanding to know what was going on.

"My bulldozer," explained John Larkman. "Her yard. No problem."

Sophie wanted to grow up and settle major issues in six words.

Mr. Larkman said it was time to kill Ted now, but Mrs. Larkman claimed to like Ted a little bit and suggested locking him in the cellar for a few years instead.

"I forbid punishment of Ted," said Edith. "I bear full responsibility."

"It's about time," said John Larkman. "You gonna go all out and get a job in January?"

"Yes," said Edith. "And with my half of the money, I'll buy a nice house to live in. Sophie and I want a place to hear music."

Dad was looking at his former wife with what Sophie thought was affection and possibly even respect. Then he looked at Sophie for a long deep time, as if seeing her from crib to driver's license. But nobody was looking at Daniel. They had turned their backs on him to gather around Edith; they were a row of backs—backs of heads, backs of shoulders, backs of elbows and backs of knees.

And really, at this stage, there was no going back.

"Climb in the dump truck, everybody," said John Larkman. "It's almost midnight. We're gonna finish our solstice in style. I didn't carry all those hay bales up there for nothing."

"Good-bye, Dad," said Sophie politely. "Have a nice trip. Don't forget the postcards."

•——\/\/\/\——•

And so the soap opera left the air.

It was entirely possible that Daniel and Persia and Edith would remain onstage, endlessly clashing; always forgetting the lesson they had learned last week, the way people did on television soaps— year in, year out, the same enemy crushing the same good guy.

But Sophie was not a character in her own soap opera.

She had survived, and survival was the act of reaching the last episode.

It began to snow.

Sophie and Ted walked.

Snow fell between them and on them. They tilted their heads back and the snow frosted their eyelashes and lay cold and tasty on their lips. Ted took her mitten off and wrapped his hand around her fingers instead. He was freezing in his tuxedo and he didn't even care. Her warm hand was enough to warm his soul.

"I wanted Edith to take the tower down," said Ted.

"She took Daniel down. That was what mattered to her."

Ted looked to see what mattered to Sophie.

It turned out to be him.

It took a long time to reach the circle. When they finally arrived, the stones were shouldered in snow, and there was no trace of a party. They henged one complete circle, and they henged another, and then they lay on their backs in the snow, and the snow stopped falling. The sky cleared. The stars looked down.

"Sophie?" said Ted. "Will you be my date for the New Year?"

She was melting the snow beneath her. She and Ted would leave their outlines here. "The evening it begins?" said Sophie, staring at the universe. "Or the whole year?"

Ted breathed in for a long time. Then he breathed out, taking forever. "The year," said Ted, who could not be casual.

Sophie turned her back on the stars and smiled at Ted.

They didn't take it away from me after all, thought Sophie. They can let love die. They can throw love away. But I can still have a love of my own.